CATS ON THE RUN!

CATS ON THE RUN!

by

GED GILLMORE

www.gedgillmore.com

Cataloguing-in-Publication details are available from the National Library of Australia www.trove.nla.gov.au

ISBN 978-0-9941786-0-2

Cover illustration: Ace Connell.
Cover design: Spiffing Covers.
Editing: Anne Greenberg, Helen Masterton.
Copy Editing: Verushka Byrow.
Proofing: Verushka Byrow.
Set in Times New Roman.

10987654321

Printed: Lightning Source (Worldwide)

This is a work of fiction. Names, characters, businesses, places, events and incidents are either the products of the author's imagination or used in a fictitious manner. Any resemblance to actual persons, witches, cats or poodles, living or dead, or actual events is purely coincidental.

I would like to express my humble thanks to my teachers and fellow students at the Bronte Writers' Studio, for sharing their own personal witchcraft.

I wrote down this story for
Hellie
to make her laugh.

Her guidance and support made it possible to turn the
story into a book and for that I will be forever grateful.

But I must dedicate *Cats On The Run* to
Oliver
for he makes everything else possible.

WARNING!

This is the story of some cats I know and the frankly horrible things that happened to them last year. How they got what they thought they wanted, and how it nearly killed them. But before I begin the story, I need to confirm you're up to hearing the ghastly events it contains. Are you tough enough? Are you rough enough? Are you downright gruff enough? If not, I recommend you put this book down right now and go back to your colouring-in, you big baby. Continue only if you are up for a Big Action Drama (B.A.D.) book. It's rough, tough, and ain't got no fluff. Are you down with that? Are you up for it? Have you looked left and right? OK, here we go.

THE FIRST BIT

Once upon a time there were two cats, and their names were Tuck and Ginger. Ginger was a ginger cat (surprise!); she had thick, striped fur; six bellies; and could say 'miaow' in seven languages. She'd been around the block a few times, Ginger had, and she didn't mind telling you about it. For example, you might be picking your nose when you thought no one was looking, and Ginger, appearing from nowhere, would tell you about a boy she once knew in New York who picked his nose so hard his brain came out on the end of his finger.

Or you might say you'd just got back from Tibet. 'Pah!' Ginger would say. 'Tibet! It's all cheap sheep and chirpy Sherpas.' She was so well travelled, you see, so experienced, so been-there-done-that, that not a lot impressed her. Not that Ginger showed off. Oh baloney, no. She didn't think she was superior for having had such a varied and—as you'll learn—hard life. But she didn't hide it either. Ginger didn't often go skydiving these days, but everyone knew she could do it.

Now, Tuck couldn't be any more different. This, as you'll find out, is both a good and a bad thing. Most things are both good and bad, have you noticed that? What's the nastiest thing in the world, for example?

Personally, I'd say poo is probably the most horrible thing in the world. But, hey, if there was no poo then all the food you'd ever eaten would still be inside your body, sitting there, gassy and rotting, and washing about your insides. You'd look like a politician!

Anyhoo, Tuck was a very different cat from Ginger. Firstly, he was born in a refugee camp, which has no direct bearing on this story but is interesting because it was a refugee camp built for dogs. Tuck grew up in a little cage in the cat room, which the camp management had been forced to set up for the cat refugees who kept arriving. For the first year of his life Tuck knew nothing of the outside world. All he heard—morning, noon, and night—was the howling of abandoned dogs. Is there a lonelier or sadder sound in the world? (Here's a clue: no.)

Now, whether it was this strange upbringing that sent Tuck slightly loop-the-loop or some other factor, we will never know. The point is that Tuck was a little, how shall I put it? Well, you decide: Tuck was the kind of cat who would interrupt a conversation to ask how much a broom costs. Or he might tell you that Santa doesn't employ fairies because fairies don't exist. Tuck had four different favourite colours. He believed in ghosts and liked to talk to them in the litter tray. You get the picture? He was one crazy cat.

But Tuck was also a real athlete. You might call him a lean, mean, fighting machine, except he mostly lacked the courage to fight anyone but Ginger. Unlike Ginger, Tuck had no fat on him at all. When he was chasing string, you could see the muscles ripple under his coat, and his belly was as firm as a brand-new tennis ball. Tuck was black, as black as a panther. His fur, nose, whiskers, the pads on the bottom of his feet and even his claws were all pitch-black. Naturally, this was something of which Tuck was very proud. The only things about Tuck that weren't black were his razor-sharp teeth (sparkly white), his sandpaper tongue (pink), and his amazing hunter's eyes (green or yellow, depending on his mood). In the dark, Tuck's body disappeared completely, and all you could see were those huge flashing eyes and (if he was smiling), all those white teeth. He was like a Masai warrior, proud and stealthy in the night but scared of vacuum cleaners.

Inevitably, there were fights. Oh boy, did Tuck and Ginger fight! Have you ever heard of the expression 'the fur will fly'? You haven't? You should get out more and talk to people; it's a very common expression.

Anyhoo, when these cats fought, the fur would definitely fly—huge clumps of black or ginger cat hair wafting through the apartment where the two of them lived. If Tuck found Ginger on his favourite spot on the back of the sofa, he'd pounce on her and bite her ears until he could taste wax. Or if Ginger found Tuck on the double bed upstairs, well, **hoochie baroochie**, all hell would break loose. Tuck would kick Ginger in one of her six bellies, and Ginger would bite Tuck on the back of his neck. She'd hold him in a tight half nelson with her front paws and jab him in the face with her back paws. He'd pounce on her, she'd spit at him—bish bosh, crish crash—day after day after day. No claws of course as they were both decent adult cats after all, but you could never have described the two as friends. Well, you could have, but you'd have been wrong. Ginger, you see, thought Tuck was stupid, and Tuck thought Ginger was arrogant.

Now, generally when Tuck was being Tuckish, Ginger would just roll her eyes and sigh. But last year, on the day this strange and terrifying story starts, Tuck said something that changed everything and started our furry felines on an adventure where they would have to stop fighting each other and start fighting for their lives instead.

It was towards the end of autumn, and Ginger was sitting on the windowsill of the apartment where she and Tuck lived. This apartment was on the fourteenth floor of a tower block in the middle of a huge city. The apartment had an upstairs and a downstairs, like a house, but what it did not have was a garden or even a balcony, which meant Tuck and Ginger never went outside. As a result, Ginger liked to spend the little free time she had (after eating, sitting in the litter tray, fighting Tuck, and sleeping fourteen hours a day) looking out the window.

From her windowsill Ginger would watch carefully to see what she could see. Some days she would see nothing all day—just the same sky, the same trees, the same apartment blocks down the street. On other days she'd be lucky and see people and dogs and children passing by. Best of all were the days when she saw another cat. Ginger had very good eyes in those days, and she could spot a cat from anywhere. Whenever she did, she'd wonder where it was going, what adventure it might be about to have, or what types of dead food it might find on the street. If she saw a cocky cat down on the street, she'd bristle her fur and imagine scratching him on his nose and chasing him away.

Or sometimes Ginger would see a bird. Whenever she did, she'd shudder her bottom jaw and dream of catching the little thing and eating it. But mostly she'd just sit and look out at nothing and wonder if she'd ever go outside again. For this is what Ginger wanted more than anything in the world—to breathe the air of freedom and get back to the life she'd once had.

For four years now Ginger had lived in this apartment, and not a single day had passed that she hadn't dreamt of escape. She'd calculated the distance she'd have to jump to land in the nearest treetop should a window ever be left open. She'd tried climbing into her owners' luggage whenever they packed to go away. She'd even once tried signalling to a cat she sometimes saw in another apartment block across the road. But all to no avail.

And now, as Ginger sat looking out of the window, she realised she was getting old and fat and would probably never go outside again. Six bellies took a lot of filling, and she wondered if her hunting skills were what they once had been. And of course, she wasn't as vibrant a redhead as she used to be.

Ginger tried not to let herself think this way. She tried to think of positive things, but sometimes on a sunny afternoon the only noise in the apartment (when Tuck wasn't singing) was the sound of big, gingery sighs.

Ginger's view of the outside world was better in the autumn. All but the stubbornest of leaves had fallen, and she could see through the bare branches of the trees outside the window. There, in the distance, she could just make out the edge of the city and the beginning of the countryside. If she squinted, she could make out fields and hedges; she could remember the feeling of grass beneath her paws, remember how good it tasted, remember lots of things. That morning she had just let out a long and particularly gingery sigh when Tuck came trotting along.

'I want to go to the moon,' he said. 'I have a feeling the entire thing might be made of mushroom sauce.'

Ginger looked down at him. His huge eyes were bright yellow as they reflected the pale sunlight coming through the window. Now, if you'd asked Tuck what colour his eyes were at that moment, he'd have guessed green, because they were generally green when he was happy. But there were no green leaves left to reflect green light, so he sat there, happy with yellow eyes. 'Why was Tuck happy?' I hear you ask.

I said, '"Why was Tuck happy?" I hear you ask.'
Hello?

Aha, yes, I thought you'd ask that. Well, Tuck was happy because he'd had a Big New Idea. And this made him happy for two reasons. Firstly, it annoyed Ginger. Secondly, it gave him something to think about. So, what was the Big New Idea, I hear you ask? I said . . . Oh, don't bother, I'll do it myself. What was the B.N.I.? Well, the previous night Tuck and Ginger's owners had poured mushroom sauce on their dinner. Oh, **wemjee!**

I have to tell you about Tuck and Ginger's owners!

You're going to love them! Well, hate them!

Love hating them!

They . . . Oh, look, it's going to have to wait, otherwise this story is never going to start. Remind me in a minute, will you?

So the night before this story starts (if it ever blooming well starts), after the owners had eaten their dinner, Tuck snuck into the kitchen. He wasn't allowed up on the kitchen surfaces, but he reckoned once the TV was on, it would be ages before his owners-who-I-have-to-tell-you-about would come back in to tidy up. So he jumped up and started licking their dirty plates. And what did he find there? Mmmmmushroom sauce. Yummy, yummy, yummy. Well, Tuck lapped it up, and pretty soon he had decided mushroom sauce was the best food in the whole wide world. He told this to Ginger later that same night. Do you know what he said? He said, 'I think mushroom sauce is the best food in the whole wide world.'

Of course, Ginger just ignored him. She sighed and curled up tighter in the corner of the sofa where she liked to sleep at night. Then she sighed again. She couldn't be bothered telling Tuck about grass or cream or sardines or any of the far better foods she'd tasted on her travels. She merely licked one of her paws, gave him one of her looks, and put her nose under her arm. Secretly she agreed that mushroom sauce was pretty spectacular, but she'd be a tabby before she'd admit that Tuck had spoken some truth.

And she knew he'd soon enough forget about it again.

But the next day proved her wrong. Here was Tuck, a full twelve hours later, still going on about mushroom blooming sauce. It was going to be a long day.

'If the moon is made of mushroom sauce and we went to the moon, we could have mushroom sauce whenever we wanted,' he said, looking up from the floor and ignoring Ginger's obvious disinterest. 'I really want to go to the moon.' He started singing.

'Fly me to the moon,' he sang. 'Let me walk amongst the stairs. Show me what springs look like on Jupiter's sandbars.'

Now, there was little in the world that Ginger hated more than Tuck's singing. He was often off-key and always got the words wrong. Worst of all, Tuck sang almost all the time. Ginger stuck her two front paws way out in front of her and curved her back in as much as she could. Then she stuck her bum way up in the air and wiggled her tail slightly. She was going to jump on top of Tuck from here on the windowsill and see how he felt like singing then. She was just checking her position, quivering her tail and steadying her paws, when Tuck stopped singing and said, 'Oh, by the way, the cleaning lady left the front door open.'

'What?' said Ginger.

'She left the front door open. I saw into the corridor. It's got a carpet which is very close to two of my favourite blues.'

Now Ginger did jump. But not onto Tuck, for that would be a waste of valuable time. Instead she jumped to the floor and ran full speed towards the front door of the apartment. It was indeed ajar.

'Oh, sweet Tabatha,' she said.

'It's a kind of a pastel blue,' said Tuck, who had followed her. 'Or maybe cornflower. But cornflower's flowerier . . . Oh, look—a fly!'

With that he ran off, chasing the fly into the kitchen and leaving Ginger transfixed by the open door. Tentatively, without shifting from her spot, Ginger put her head forward and sniffed the air in the blue-carpeted corridor outside the apartment door.

Now, wasn't there something you were supposed to remind me about? What was it?

Oh yes! Tuck and Ginger's owners! You're going to love them, hate them . . . oh, have we done that bit? OK, here we go.

As far as the outside world was concerned, Rodney and Janice Burringo led very normal lives. They lived in an apartment with their two cats, shopped once a week at the supermarket, and went to office jobs which no one really understood.

Have you ever noticed that, by the way? No one really completely gets what anyone else does all day. It's weird, even if people used to do something themselves, they don't get what it's like when anyone else does. Like when you come home from school and your mum or dad or resident adult says, 'How was school today?' Next time they do that, I suggest you say, 'Did you ever go to school?' and when they say, 'Yes', you can say, 'Well, it was like that'. Then you can get on with picking your scabs and drawing pictures rather than answering their stupid questions.

Bennyhoo, Rodney and Janice Burringo were not normal people and did not lead normal lives. They only pretended to go to work. As soon as no one was looking, they'd sneak back to their apartment and sleep all day in the secret-upstairs-locked room that even the cats weren't allowed in. (Ginger had been caught in there once and was so severely punished that Tuck trembled just passing by the door.) The secret-upstairs-locked room was a very dark room with no windows. It contained nothing but a clothes rail where Rodney and Janice would hang their work clothes so they could sleep naked on the floor. They had to do this because in reality Rodney and Janice were . . .

Wait for it . . .

Can you guess?

No, not vampires! What is it with everyone and vampires these days? Get over the vampires thing already, it's *so* last season. No, Rodney and Janice Burringo were *witches*! Evil, nasty witches. What do you mean, men can't be witches? Get out of here with your outdated prejudices. Men and women can be whatever they want. And what did Rodney and Janice want? Durrh. They wanted to be witches!

You know how most people have saucepans in their kitchen cupboards? Rodney and Janice had cauldrons. You know how most people clean their house with a vacuum cleaner? Rodney and Janice did it with broomsticks (although they did keep a vacuum cleaner just because they knew Tuck was **terrrrrrified** of it— see how nasty they were?). And at night they would sneak up to the roof of their building with these broomsticks and launch themselves into the air, cackling loudly and scaring anyone who might be passing by. Then they'd fly all over town, leaving things where they shouldn't be. Rodney had a big bag of dog poo, and he'd leave little piles of it on the pavement outside doorways. Janice had a sack of litter, which she'd distribute in windblown alleyways. Witches love litter. It gives them little tingles up their warty spines, and you must be very careful not to walk along a littery road after dark in case a witch finds you there. You really don't want to be found by a witch, did you know that? And do you know why? Because witches just love children. Mostly they liked them fried, but Rodney and Janice preferred them grilled because it's a healthier way of cooking with less cholesterol. Best of all, though, for witches all over the world, is lightly steamed child in a white wine sauce.

Yummy yummy YUMMY!

It was as a result of the Burringos' activities that Ginger and Tuck had so much time to themselves. At night Rodney and Janice would be flying all over the city doing their dastardly deeds, and during the day they'd both be fast asleep in the secret-upstairs-locked room. Now, you might be wondering why the Burringos bothered having cats at all, and that is indeed a good question. It wasn't because they'd got pets before thinking how little time they'd get to spend with them like some idiotic people do. Oh baloney no. It was because . . . well, it's an important and interesting story, which I will tell you. But in the meantime, let's get back to Ginger.

THE FIRST AND A HALF BIT

W here were we? Oh yes. Tuck is chowing down on a fly in the kitchen, and Ginger is still standing at the apartment door. The open apartment door. How did I put it last time? 'Ginger sat transfixed by the open door'—something like that. Well, tentatively, without shifting from her spot, Ginger put her head forward and sniffed the air in the blue-carpeted corridor outside the apartment. It didn't smell like freedom. It smelled like dried baby-sick and cleaning fluids. To you or me it would just have smelled a bit fusty, but cats have got the most amazing noses, and they can be much more precise than us. As far as Ginger could tell, there was some 2006 carpet cleaner with hints of burnt-out light bulb. And baby-sick of course. The baby-sick must have been ancient, as Tuck and Ginger hadn't heard Baby crying next door for years now. I wonder what happened to him?

Bendyway, Ginger sniffed the air again until she thought, 'What am I doing? I'm still standing here like a scaredy-cat when I should be out there like a brave-cat.' Still, she didn't move. She realised she was terrified, and it was this very realisation that drove her forward. For Ginger knew that the difference between brave-cats and scaredy-cats isn't fear. It's how you act.

Brave-cats feel the fear and do it anyway. Scaredy-cats feel the fear and run like bonkers. And which do you think Ginger was?

The corridor was long and had no describable features that I haven't mentioned already. Blue carpet, fusty smell—you get the picture. It did have lots of doors leading off it, each to a different apartment, each with a different number, but these were of such a boring and bare beige I can barely bear to bring it up. The only exception was a large pair of steel double doors at the very far end of the corridor. Ginger was worried she was going to go into the corridor and not be able to get back in again. But, as stated, she was a brave-cat, and so she pushed herself forward until she heard a familiar and annoying voice behind her.

'What are you doing? Where are you going? Can I come?'

It was Tuck. He was sitting in the doorway to the apartment, licking his lips free of fly crumbs and staring out at her.

Now, unlike Ginger, Tuck had never dreamt of actually stepping outside the apartment, not even when he found the door open that morning. You see, compared to the cage he'd grown up in, the apartment was a huge and exciting world. It even had a forbidden area (the secret-upstairs-locked room) and several places he imagined only he knew about. The back of the drawers in the spare room, for example, or underneath the sideboard. The corridor might as well have been a different planet. But then again, if Ginger was going out there, he was pretty sure he wanted to go too. Heavens, if he didn't follow her out, she might think she was better than him.

'Where you going?' Tuck miaowed again.

'Ssh!' Ginger hissed back at him. 'Go upstairs. Climb on the double bed and keep it warm for me.'

Well! Now Tuck was certain he wanted to visit the corridor, for Ginger would never normally encourage him onto the bed. She was obviously up to something. So he trotted out after her, tail in the air like he just didn't care, and caught up with her at the fourth apartment door. There were only three more to pass before they'd both be at the shiny double doors at the end of the corridor.

'Ooh,' said Tuck, pointing at the shiny doors. 'What are those?'

Now, Ginger was a pretty smart cat as you might have guessed. This was why the Burringos had got her, after all. But she also had a sharp tongue, and unfortunately for her, this sharp tongue sometimes acted before her brain did.

'It's a rocket ship. You go to the moon in it. What do you think it is, you moron? It's a lift.'

'The moon!' said Tuck, his eyes flashing green as they picked up the reflection of an old curry stain in the carpet. 'I want to go to the moon!'

'I was joking,' said Ginger, who despite having four legs still couldn't actually kick herself. 'It's a lift, it's dangerous, and it's full of vacuum cleaners.'

Tuck looked unconvinced, but just then the two of them heard a strange rumbling noise from behind the silver doors.

'Oh my goodness!' said Ginger. 'Let's go. Here come the vacuum cleaners!'

Tuck was halfway back to the apartment door before he noticed Ginger wasn't running that way too. He turned round and what did he see? Ginger had actually run the other way, *towards* the silver doors. And now he could see her sitting just to the right of them as they opened and an elderly female human emerged, hobbling into the corridor. Then, as he watched in amazement, Ginger slunk into the empty lift. Now, normally Tuck would have been terrified by all of this because he was in general terrified of everything. But today as the old lady got closer, he found his fear was completely cancelled out by his fury that Ginger had tricked him. He'd been right to look unconvinced when she'd talked about the vacuum cleaners! Now she was going to the moon, and she was going to have as much mushroom sauce as she wanted, and she wasn't going to take him with her! Where do bogies go to have fun? Snot fair!

'Nooooo!' Tuck yelled as he ran at his almost absolute fastest the full length of the corridor.

Have I mentioned what an amazing and beautiful athlete Tuck is? Boy, can he move when he puts his mind to it. This is why he was brave enough to fight Ginger, because he always knew he could outrun her if she ever got the upper paw (which she always did). But he'd never run faster than he did now. Later in the story he does, he runs plenty faster, believe you me, but for now this was the fastest he'd ever run. The little old lady barely had time to say, 'What a sweet little—' before

Tuck had passed between her hundred-year-old ankles. Apartment doors flew by in a ballistic blur of bland and boring beige as he bombed along the corridor, the wind in his ears and his cheeks flapping from the G-force.

Ginger heard him coming. 'Oh no,' she thought. She'd planned on waiting for the doors of the elevator to close automatically, so she could float down to the ground floor sedately like a lady. Now she jumped up as high as she could to try to press the G button or any button to get the lift doors to close as quickly as possible.

Damn these six bellies, she thought.

In her heyday she could knock a milk bottle off a high shelf. Now she barely made it to the lowest button. At last she gave a mighty, huge, slow-motion jump with special-effects sounds **(wacker tacker tacker tacker tacker)** and head-butted the >|< button to close the doors. They started closing slowly.

But Ginger had taken too long and Tuck was too fast. He bounded between the closing doors in an even slower-motion dive than Ginger had managed. Can you imagine the background music to that? Then he landed right on top of Ginger so that they rolled in a black-and-ginger ball into the corner of the lift.

'No!' said Ginger. 'No, no, no!'

'Yes,' said Tuck. 'Yes, yes, yes! We're going to the moon, mushroom moon, mushmoon sauce wheee!'

Then he said, 'Are we there yet?'

This might be a good time to tell you why the Burringos got themselves two cats in the first place. I mean, nothing much happens to Tuck and Ginger for the next couple of hours. They just sit and wait for a long, long time to travel to the ground floor slash moon. Every so often Tuck asks how much longer it will take to get there, but apart from that they just take turns peeing in the corner. Very dull. Unless you're really into watching cats wee in corners, in which case . . . Oh, never mind. I may as well just tell you how Tuck and Ginger ended up with the evil, child-grilling Burringos in the first place.

It was Janice Burringo's idea. You see, as you may or may not know, witches generally own very clever black cats. Like anything else, these come in all shapes and sizes. For the really rich witch who works hard at school and saves lots of money the absolute crème de la crème of cats is a pure black Purrari. These are famously hard to come by and, as the laws of supply and demand dictate, are extremely expensive. If you and your brothers and sisters and all your cousins and everyone you know saved up all their pocket money for the rest of their lives, you still could never afford one. That's how expensive they are. But unfortunately, Janice Burringo had expensive tastes. She liked fancy dresses and good restaurants, crystal glasses, and silky undies. If this was a fairy story, she'd be a confusing character because she would be both a witch and a princess. But this is not a fairy story. It's a gritty tale of life on the streets, and Janice was all witch and a greedy one at that. Oh, how she wanted a black Purrari.

When Janice first met Rodney Burringo, back in the days when she was plain Janice Phaniss, she thought he would be the man to give her everything she wanted in life. She was one of those misguided people who think you should marry someone for reasons other than love. Rodney, she thought, had potential. So she ditched her then-boyfriend, Richard Branson, and took up instead with Rodney Burringo, who looked like he was made for money. Well, can you guess what happened?

That's right! Rodney was not made for money. Rodney was far too sensible for that. A couple of years after they were married, Rodney realised that making money (which he could do only by staying indoors and slaving all night over a smelly, steaming cauldron) was not half as much fun as leaving dog poo in awkward places on pavements. And what was the point of making money if it stopped him doing the things he loved? So Rodney spent as little time as possible with the smelly cauldron and as much time as possible with the dog poo. It's an interesting choice, I know, but hey, it takes all sorts.

Now, you might be wondering what all this has to do with Tuck and Ginger. But hang in there—it has everything to do with them. You see, Janice's major downfall in life was a rare condition known in the medical profession as Being a Completely Lazy Slob. And Janice was the laziest lazy slob you can imagine. It's why she was, like all truly evil people, so stick thin. She might have been a bit curvier, but, you see, she was too blooming lazy to chase children for more than the first hundred metres or so. After that she'd give up and bite her nails instead and watch the poor little mites run screaming into the distance. And she certainly wasn't going to put all that effort in over a smelly, steaming cauldron to cook up an alternative. Oh big bogies no. She and Rodney ate children less than they did beans on toast or soup out of a can or sometimes cat food because (a) it was in the house anyway and (b) it's so easy to prepare.

Let this be a lesson to you folks. Laziness is the most terrible, horrible thing in the world. It sucks you dry and leaves you dissatisfied. And that's what Janice was. Dissatisfied. Oh, how she wanted things to be different. She wanted to live in a house, not an apartment. She wanted fancy dresses. She wanted lots of things. But she was too lazy to do anything but complain.

As for Rodney, he was fine. He loved his life, but what was he to do? Make himself unhappy just to keep his lazy, greedy partner satisfied? Many otherwise normal people would do that, but was Rodney an otherwise normal person? He was not. He was a witch! Any part of that unclear?

Right then: cats. This was Janice Burringo's idea. Clearly, she and Rodney were never going to be able to afford a Purrari, so maybe, she thought, maybe they could magic themselves one.

'All we need,' she said to Rodney one night from the sofa, where she was eating chips and watching cartoons, 'is two cats. One pure black but not very clever and therefore quite cheap. And one really smart one—a ginger, for example. Then we'll just find a really good spell on Spookle and combine them.'

'What if we end up with a stupid ginger one?' said Rodney, who like most annoyingly sensible people was always aware of the potential risks in any situation. Janice tutted and threw a chip at him.

'Oh, Rodney Bodney, bidgey pidgey boo, pwease can we try it?' she said.

Now, if anyone spoke to you or me like that, we'd probably be sick in a bucket, especially if that person was warty, skinny Janice Burringo. But Rodney found this silliness irresistible. You see, even though Janice no longer loved him, Rodney thought Janice was the bee's knees. Coincidentally, one of her grandmothers had been a bee, and another one had been a knee, not that this has any bearing on this story, but it's interesting, isn't it? No? Oh, suit yourself. The point is. Rodney loved Janice very, very much.

'Go on then,' he said, secretly hoping Janice would forget all about the stupid idea of combining cats. But Janice didn't forget all about it. In fact, she did the opposite and started telling everyone that Rodney was going to buy her a Purrari for her birthday. What a silly witch she was.

Eventually, after about six months of this and a bit more pleading and a few stand-up fights, Rodney realised he'd better pull his finger out and actually do something about getting two cats. One stupid, just like Janice had said, and another very smart one. He'd heard about the dog refugee camp, so eventually, when Janice had reminded him of how much he loved her, he caught a taxi down there. Tuck was an easy choice—he was the purest, blackest cat in the whole camp and quite obviously a sandwich short of a picnic.

And how did Rodney find Ginger? Ginger was driving the taxi. Rodney tempted her up to the apartment with the promise of a good tip, a saucer of cream, and a little tummy-rubbing action, and he never let her go again. Oh, what a foul and cruel kidnapping! Even more cruel than you can now imagine, but read on and you'll understand. It was cataclysmic and categorically catastrophic, and to top it off, to this day the taxi company are after Ginger for stealing one of their vehicles.

Anyhoo, so there's Rodney with the two most perfect cats for Janice's big idea, but could he find a spell on Spookle to merge them into her perfect cat? Could he buffalo! He even asked Janice for help, and she too searched for almost a whole hour before giving up and turning on a late-night soap instead. Still, Rodney didn't give up. After all, he loved Janice and really wanted to make her happy. Also he had vague feelings of status anxiety for not being richer, and he thought having a Purrari might help with these. So he searched and searched. He wrote into *What's On Spelly?* magazine and ordered a few back issues of *Witch!* to see if he could get any ideas, but there was nothing. He found an online forum where someone suggested that there might be something in the *Hell o' Pages*, but that book had been out of print for years. Apart from that, there was apparently no spell for merging two cats into one.

So, as is the way with lazy people, Janice let the idea of the cat-merging spell drift onto the long, long list of things she would one day get around to doing like knitting, swimming on a Sunday morning, running, reading *War and Peace*. She did none of them and resigned herself to the lazy fact that Ginger and Tuck would remain as two separate and very different cats, who in the meantime needed feeding. That was until . . . Oh no, I'll tell you that in a bit. For now, let's see what our pussycat heroes are up to.

OH LOOK,
ANOTHER BIT!

Well, as I said, Ginger and Tuck, Tuck and Ginger (got to be fair here) sat in the elevator for hours, waiting for someone to press a button and bring it to the ground floor. You might have thought that in an apartment block of forty-four floors there would always be someone going up or down. But if you had thought that you'd have been **wrongedy-wrong, ding dang dong**. It was three hours before someone came along and called the lift. When they did, though, well, can you imagine the excitement for Ginger of going down in the lift? For Tuck of going up in the rocket ship? Different but equal, like so many things in life. Don't worry, I'm not going to drag this out. Movement, noise, excitement, doors opening, lobby, doors to the street, blah, blah, blah. Let's get on with the next scene, shall we?

Basically, the lift was called to the ground floor of the apartment building, and then—*ding*—it opened. Well, Ginger wasn't going to take any risks. As soon as the lift doors slid apart, she bolted out, ran between the legs of the fat man waiting for the lift and bolted for the street. As you can imagine, Tuck was not about to get left behind. No matter how much he wanted to go to the moon, he was still a scaredy-cat, after all. Besides, he was worried Ginger might lick up all the mushroom sauce before he could get any. It was easy for him to keep up with Ginger. He was an athlete, after all, and sooner than you can say, 'Oh look, two sweet pussycats running across the foyer of a large apartment building', they were outside. Out in the real world at last. Except of course Tuck thought it was the moon.

Ginger breathed in the air of the city street. She'd forgotten how... well, not to put too fine a point on it, she'd forgotten how smelly it smelled. Exhaust fumes, rubbish bins, hundreds of people farting and burping along the street. Yummy yummy YUMMY! The Burringos had a very good cleaner (when she wasn't leaving doors open), and their apartment always smelled of light but effective cleaning products and a variety of flowers (the cleaner, a lady by the name of Arthur, always brought flowers to her employers' apartments). But down here, down on the street, it smelled different. It smelled real. It smelled earthy.

Tuck smelled it too, but of course the smell was completely new to him. The refugee camp where he had grown up had only ever really smelled of dog. Here smelled of everything. A hundred different things he couldn't name. It was exciting and new and utterly terrifying.

'Wh-wh-where are you going?' Tuck asked as Ginger trotted, tail in the air like she just didn't care, down the path between the front door of the apartment block and the pavement.

'Away,' said Ginger. 'Away from here, away from you. Away, away, away.'

Tuck pretended not to hear and kept close to her side. He wasn't sure he liked the moon as much as he'd thought he would. So far there was no mushroom sauce in sight.

'No way,' said Ginger, suddenly staring at something on the road in front of them.

Tuck looked at her and then followed her gaze to see what she had seen.

And what had she seen?

Well, what Ginger had seen was nothing short of a miracle. What Ginger had seen was something she had given up hope of ever seeing again. She picked up her pace across the pavement, Tuck still keeping up with her, and then stopped no more than a metre away from her old taxi. It sat there, with its tiger-stripe pattern, chugging away and wobbling like a giant jelly next to the kerb, putt-putt-putting fumes out of its old exhaust pipe. Pretty impressive after four years, I know, but that's those new hybrids for you.

'It's still here!' said Ginger.

Tuck watched as she jumped up into the taxi and then followed double-quick. He wasn't going to be left on the pavement of the moon all by himself without any mushroom sauce.

Ginger jumped up and down on each of the seats, looking under them, exploring the taxi as if searching for something. After a minute or two, she seemed to give up her search and sighed a big, deep, ginger sigh.

Well, it was a long, long time (four years actually) since Ginger had driven a taxi, and of course Tuck never had driven one. But Ginger thought this was too good an opportunity to miss, so she told Tuck what to do. She made him jump down to the pedals and showed him which one was the brake and which was the accelerator (there were only two pedals because—**durrh**—cats can drive only automatics). Ginger pushed the car into Drive, which was easier than it used to be now that she was fatter, and she was about to take off the handbrake when something caught her eye. It was a single ginger hair, down on the carpet next to Tuck. Paler than her own coat, it looked like it had been there for years.

'What is it?' said Tuck.

'Nothing...' Ginger murmured after a while. 'Nothing at all. Now jump on the accelerator. Gently!'

It was a stop-start journey as you can imagine if you've ever tried driving with a cat that's not had lessons. Tuck wasn't good with his left and right at the best of times, and he slowed them down at the first few green lights and sped up at the red ones. But after a while, and much to Ginger's surprise, he got the hang of it. 'Goodness,' thought Ginger, 'I must be instructing him very well.'

As for her, well, her job was easy. Once you learn a city as well as Ginger had learnt this one you never forget. She took them right off Rawley Road and into Railway Square, then north across the square and into Long Lane. Along Long Lane and down around the roundabout and fast past the park. Oh yes, folks, Ginger knew the city pretty well, and soon enough she and Tuck were putting some distance between themselves and the Burringos' apartment.

THE SECOND BIT

Did you wonder why Arthur the cleaning lady left the apartment door open? I mean, she'd been cleaning that flat for at least four years, and she'd never done it before. So why now? Well, let me tell you. Rodney and Janice were not only lazy at being witches, they were lazy at other things too. Like cleaning up the kitchen after they'd had dinner or writing thank-you notes after birthdays or picking up the wages for their cleaning lady. Arthur, you see, liked to be paid in cash. She had a deep distrust of banks and kept all her money in a big box under her bed. So every Tuesday, when she arrived at the Burringos' apartment, the first thing she'd do was make sure they'd left her **one hundred doodahs** on the kitchen counter. And often they hadn't. This used to drive Arthur nuts.

'Agh!' she'd scream. 'It drives me nuts.'

Well, on the day this story starts, the day she left the door open, Arthur decided she'd had it up to here with the Burringos. No cash on the kitchen counter again. 'Enough!' she said. 'Those blasted bothersome Burringos are too mean. I'm not a machine! They can find someone else to wash and clean.' And she flounced out, her big bottom wobbling as she stomped out of the apartment and down the corridor toward the lift. She was so angry she even left the door open behind her— this being much classier and dramatic than slamming it. Arthur didn't care if the cats escaped, for she had decided she was Never Going to Clean for the Burringos again. Serves them right whatever happens. So there. Humph!

Well. Can you imagine the scene that evening when Janice and Rodney woke up in their windowless room? At first it was normal. Janice put on her fluffy slippers and the tracksuit she liked to wear around the house, and Rodney stretched and shaved himself, using the fin of a shark he'd once caught. And then they went downstairs.

'Eugh,' said Rodney. 'The apartment's still dirty'.

'Ooch,' said Janice. 'There's a horrible breeze coming through the apartment door.'

And then they both said, 'Where are the cats?'

You see, they might have never got round to turning their two cats into a Purrari, but they'd never given up on the idea. And besides, witches are extremely possessive. Once they think they own something they get **fuuuuuu- uuuuuuuuuuuuuuuuuuuuuuuuuuurious** if it gets taken away from them.

Have you ever smelled a furious witch? It's not good. It's a bit like a cocktail of cabbage and vomit with a hint of something you trod in. And when witches are emotional in any way, they don't look great either. Their eyes turn bright red. Have you ever seen a photo of someone and the flash has put a little red dot in their eye? Well, that's what witches' eyes look like when they're angry. As if that wasn't enough, their skin gets a greenish tinge, and their noses get little bumps on them before hooking over.

Then—**PING!**—their chins stick out. All those pictures you've seen of witches, they're always angry in them.

'I'm going to find those cats,' said Rodney, 'and I'm going to skin them alive!'

'I'm going to cook them slowly,' said Janice. 'I'll whisk their whiskers, sear their ears, boil their tails, and pause only before paring their paws.'

Eugh, horrible, horrible witches. I'll bet you thought Janice and Rodney were a bit harmless, didn't you? Not a bit of it. Once they'd filled the apartment with such a stench of anger that even they couldn't bear to stay there, they ran up and put on their witching outfits, and then they opened up the living room window extra wide and flew out into the city night, cackling loudly and leaving a toxic trail of nastiness behind them.

'Let's find those horrible little cats!' they screamed. 'Let's make them pay!'

So where were our feline friends while this was happening? Well, they were still in the taxi, but were they chugging full speed away from the city to safety? They were not. And why not? Come on, guess. Work it out. No? Well, I'd better tell you then. They'd run out of petrol. Not surprising really. I mean the taxi had been waiting on the kerb for four years. Only an hour after Tuck and Ginger had driven off, the car started making strange noises. **Chuggedy-chuggedy-phut-phut**, that kind of thing. Never good in a car. Well, Ginger directed Tuck on the pedals, and she steered to where she could coast downhill, but shortly before dark the car went **phutty-phutty-churg-churg** and died. Just like that. It was partly by luck and partly by Ginger's skill that they were in a quiet, little side street when it happened. Ginger leaned on the steering wheel so that the big old taxi curved towards the pavement and came to a rest in a perfect parallel-park position.

'What do we do now?' said Tuck.

'We stop asking questions,' said Ginger.

'Why do we do that?'

'I tell you what,' said Ginger, 'why don't you get out and walk down the road a bit and sing a song?'

Now, if Ginger told you and me to do that, we'd probably tell her to get lost, but Tuck thought it was actually a very good idea. Without a second thought he jumped out of the window and trotted down the tarmac a couple of metres. Then a couple of metres more, until he was sure he was out of earshot. He looked up at the fading sky and started to sing:

'Oh moon, oh moon,
Forgive my tune-
lessness. I didn't expect to be here so soon.
I can't complain, it is a boon.

'It's great of course.
I like it of course.
I just wish we could find
All your mushroom sauce.'

Songs had never been Tuck's strong suit.

Meanwhile, Ginger sat down on the taxi's driver's seat and wondered what they were going to do for their supper. Outside it was getting darker by the minute, and it was the time of day when Ginger's bellies always started rumbling and demanding some food. Can you remember how many bellies Ginger has? Six. And let me tell you, it takes more than the whiff of mint air freshener to fill six bellies. But a whiff of mint air freshener was all there was in the car, and even that was four years old. Ho-hum.

But Ginger didn't mind being hungry—it wouldn't be the first time it had happened to her—and besides, she was free. Free for the first time in years. So very sensibly (and you'll discover that Ginger was a very sensible cat) she decided to enjoy her freedom first of all and worry about food in the morning. She made herself comfortable by curling up extra tight in the driver's seat, the end of her tail over her nose, and watched the sky grow black outside the taxi windows. Soon she was fast asleep and snoring and snuffling like a little pot-bellied pig.

I don't know if you've ever noticed this, but some people are morning people and some people are evening people. Morning people just love the mornings. They jump out of bed, singing, and they race out to enjoy the sunshine and pick the flowers. Evening people generally hate mornings. They hate them almost as much as they hate morning people in the mornings. Evening people spend the mornings saying things like 'Not before my coffee' and 'Go away'. They think morning people are annoying, but in return morning people think evening people are grumpy. And it's not equal on both sides. Oh no. Morning people mourn evening people's morning behaviour far more than evening people mourn morning people's evening behaviour. Obviously.

Now, do you know which you are? Are you annoying or grumpy? Well, Ginger was definitely a morning cat. She liked to rise early, do her yoga, and clean her claws whilst listening to the birds sing and imagining what they tasted like. Tuck, of course, was the polar opposite. He was very much an evening cat. If you tried talking to Tuck before about 10:00 a.m., he'd look like he was listening to you, but in fact, all he would be thinking would be 'Shut up, shut up, shut up'. So at this point in the story, where Ginger was settling down for the night, Tuck was really waking up. Once he'd sung his first song to the moon, he sang another two, which were frankly even sillier than the first, so I won't bother repeating them. Let's just say he got to rhyming 'sauce' with 'horse', and as you know, cats don't like horses.

Anyweeway, once Tuck had finished singing, he decided to see if anyone wanted to play. He knew Ginger long enough to know she'd be asleep by now, so he didn't bother asking her. Instead, as the stars plinked on high above him and the streetlights plinked on a little lower down, he looked behind rubbish bins and under cars, on top of a pile of bricks and even under a bush to see if there was anyone, anyone at all on the moon who wanted to play. But there was nobody.

Poor Tuck. He was feeling a bit despondent and

lonely, trying ever so hard to like the moon but finding it very dull, when suddenly he saw a movement out of the corner of his eye. At first he thought it might be just his own shadow. He'd been caught out that way before. So he stood as still as a still thing and waited. And there was the movement again. Tuck stared with the superb night-vision goggles which all cats wear inside their heads and saw a little twitchy nose and a pair of little twitchy ears appear from a hole in the gutter which he hadn't noticed before. Soon the ears and nose were followed by a furry, grey body.

'A mouse!' said Tuck. 'Hello, mouse! Do you want to play? Do you want to play catch?'

Well, whether the little rodent thought this was a good idea or not we'll never know, because he just turned and ran full speed in the opposite direction. He went *squeak, squeak, squeak* as he scampered along the gutter. Then he went *squawk!* as Tuck caught up with him in two easy bounds and sank his shiny, white teeth into the back of the rodent's neck. Tuck wasn't quite sure why he'd done that, but it sure was fun.

'Ooh, ooh, ooh,' he thought. 'Let's see if there's another one and I can do it again.'

Meanwhile, on the other side of town, Janice and Rodney were circling slowly above a deserted playground. This was partly because Janice had run out of breath and partly because Rodney was savouring the scent of small innocents that still hung in the air above the concrete.

'**Ooffee**,' said Janice. 'I'm more extremely exhausted than an exhumed executive. Maybe we should go home and order a takeaway instead of looking for these silly cats.'

'What?' said Rodney. 'Are you crazy? And let those miserable little creatures make fools of us? No way. It's only just got dark. I'll bet that's when they'll take their chances, and it'll be easier for us to find them.'

But even Rodney had to admit that finding two medium-size cats in a very large-size city needed a bit of planning. And of course he wasn't wrong. If you ever want to do anything difficult—and the difficult things are the only ones worth doing—then you always need a plan. Or at the very least a list, which is really just a simple plan if you think about it. So Rodney told Janice they could sit down on the next flat roof they found.

'Let's think,' he said when they'd parked on the red roof of Rufus's Rare Roofing Supplies. 'They'll be trying to get as far from us as possible as quickly as they can. How would they do that?'

'On a plane,' said Janice, who was very possibly being sarcastic. They say sarcasm is the lowest form of wit, but I'm not sure that's true. Either way, Janice's comment gave Rodney an idea.

'Or a car,' he said. 'A car! Hang on, when we left tonight, was that big tiger-striped taxi outside like normal? I don't remember seeing it.'

'No!' said Janice. 'It was definitely gone. And that's the taxi Ginger was driving when we got her. That's it—they must be in the taxi!'

And so the Burringos decided that instead of looking for two cats (which are rather small), they should look for one big tiger-striped taxi (which is rather big and tiger-striped). 'Ha ha,' they cackled. 'Mwah ha ha ha ha! Those cats haven't got a chance!' And they flew into the air, trailing orange and green smoke out of their bottoms, which is an embarrassing phenomenon that happens to overexcited witches. They flew over all the suburbs in the south and west of the city. Which is fortunate, really, because of course, our furry, fleeing, feline friends had headed exactly north-east.

GOSH, ANOTHER BIT ALREADY

Ginger awoke with the daylight. At first she couldn't quite remember where she was. She'd had troubled dreams of distant thunder and booming seas, no doubt caused by the rumbly grumbling of her six bellies. 'Mmm,' she thought at first. 'Maybe another five minutes sleep before I have to wake up and really be hungry.' Which just goes to show how hungry she was because morning cats normally jump out of bed as soon as they can.

But then Ginger remembered why she was hungry. She was free! She had escaped! Whoopee doobie dingbats! She sat bolt upright, suddenly ready for the day. She scratched a little behind her right ear with her hind leg, looked up through the windscreen at the blue sky above and listened to the birds chirruping from the overhead power lines. But birds, of course, made her think of food. Oh, what she wouldn't give now for a tiny tin of tuna chunks. Freedom was good—the air smelled fresh with old fish bones and distant dustbins wafting on the breeze—but, oh Budapest, was she the capital of hungry.

Tuck was fast asleep on the passenger seat, snoring his flat snores. He was incapable of being in tune even when asleep. Ginger looked down at him and tutted. She didn't notice the bits of grey fur around his mouth or the dirty hairs which bent inwards as he inhaled, then outwards as he let out his snore. She was too hungry to think about anything but food. She jumped onto the dashboard and walked past the steering wheel to the open driver-side window and was about to jump down onto the tarmac when she saw the most amazing sight. 'I'm dreaming,' she said to herself out loud. She pinched herself—not easy when you don't have opposable digits—and it hurt, but there she was still, wide-awake, looking down at not one, not two, but six full-size rats laid out on the tarmac next to the car.

'Miaow!' she said. 'Tuck, Tuck, wake up. Do you know anything about this?'

Tuck, not being a morning cat, didn't respond at first, so Ginger jumped onto the seat next to him so that it bounced him up and down until he had to open his eyes.

'What do you know about the rats outside?' Ginger said.

'Sleeping,' said Tuck.

'You can sleep when you tell me about the rats. What happened?'

'I was playing dicey micey, but none of them were any good, and then they were dead, so I thought you'd know what to do with them. Can I sleep now?'

Could he sleep now?! He could sleep like Sleeping Beauty for a hundred years if he wanted to! Ginger felt like kissing him, but of course she never would. Instead she jumped back up onto, through, and down from the window in a flow as graceful as any cat with six bellies could ever manage. Then she ran along the still-cold road to the back of the taxi and opened the boot. It was **chocka-blocka** full of her old possessions. Crammed to the edges with things she hadn't seen for four years: beach balls, boxing gloves, a dirty biscuit tin with suspicious contents, a Hula Hoop, and a decent selection of red wines. But she ignored all of these. Instead she reached in and pulled out from its trusty bottom-left position a camping stove and then—top right—a frying pan.

'Oh yeah, baby,' she said. 'Ratatouille for breakfast.'

Ginger had learnt to cook on a container ship in the South China Sea, where—as you may or may not know—rat dishes are a serious speciality. Unfortunately, Ginger had to leave the vessel after a disagreement with the head cook (an absolute dragon) in Shanghai harbour. But she'd left with an amazing knowledge of rodent cuisine. Pest-o sauce, sliced mice, vole-au-vents, flying-foxtail soup, diced-mice rice, and of course, ratatouille.

No more than ten minutes after Ginger had awoken, even Tuck was happy to open his eyes and face the day, for the aroma of fried rat guts filled the air around the taxi. Can you imagine anything more mouth-watering than freshly cooked rat guts? With a salsa of diced tails on a bed of wilted ears?

Yummy yummy YUM-YUMS!

Tuck sat on the bonnet of the taxi, rubbing his eyes as Ginger—who had also found herself an old apron and floppy chef's hat—tossed the entrails in the frying pan.

She had a long piece of grass hanging out of one corner of her mouth and was very possibly smiling.

'Are the mice ready to eat yet?' said Tuck.

'Rats,' said Ginger. 'They're rats, you . . . you . . . silly thing.'

She couldn't bring herself to call him a moron just yet. He had, after all, provided their breakfast. And it suddenly occurred to her that, if she took him along, he might continue to provide food for the long journey which lay ahead.

Back on the other side of town were two very deflated witches. I mean literally deflated—all that colourful bum gas really does take it out of you. Again, literally. Rodney and Janice, never fond of the daylight at the best of times, had barely made it home before the evil energy they required to fly their broomsticks ran out completely. They were miserable, saggy, and very, very tired. They dragged themselves up to their windowless room, dropped their black robes to the floor, threw their pointy hats into the corner, and collapsed naked onto the floorboards.

'Oooh,' wailed Janice. 'I'm soooo tired.'

' ,' said Rodney, who really was beyond words. In fact, he was already asleep and dreaming. He dreamt of the life that could have been, of a big castle on a desolate mountain, with Janice happy and beautiful with a top-of-the-range broomstick and a sleek black Purrari beside her. He dreamt of himself flying alongside her into the city, throwing litter and dog poo in all directions. They were laughing and in love with life, all soft focus and cootchie-cootchie-coo.

But the trouble with nice dreams is that you have to wake up from them. Horrible dreams are much better, and nightmares are best. Then you wake up and think, 'Phew! Thank goodness I didn't really steal a shark from the aquarium and put it in my teacher's bath and get double detention. Life is sweet after all!' But if you wake up from a wonderful dream like Rodney did, well. The deep, dreary, and downright dull disappointment is doubly depressing. But Rodney was not a man to take things lying down. Oh baloney no. So when he awoke that evening he stood up.

'No,' he said. Just that, nothing else. 'No!'

He was going to find those two cats if it was the last thing he ever did. He left Janice still asleep and drooling onto the floorboards, went downstairs, and found a map of the city. He crossed off all the suburbs he and Janice had visited already and then planned where they would go that night. They'd been south and they'd been west. Tonight, Rodney decided, they would head directly north-east and scour each and every street in search of a big tiger-striped taxi. First, though, he'd have to re-motivate and re-energise his darling wife.

Rodney searched through the kitchen to see what he could find to make her as an afternoon-tea-slash-breakfast treat. In the back of the fridge he found an old pair of fingers, which—once he'd scraped out the rot from under the nails—he threw into the blender with a mango and some ice cubes. Then he poured in the end of a box of pus, which was well past its smell-by date but didn't look too bad, and whizzed the whole lot together.

He poured the blood-and-yellow concoction into Janice's favourite Knickerbocker glory glass and carried it upstairs to her on a tray, alongside the new issue of *Witch!* magazine unopened in its cellophane cover.

'You deserve a lie-in and some pampering for being such an absolute witch,' he told Janice as she sat up and stretched. 'You take it easy, honey-bunny. You stay here and take care of yourself while I go and find those cats.'

Janice, of course, was delighted to be woken up by a cold finger smoothie.

'Oh, Rodney Bodney,' she said, slurping it down. 'I can't let you do that. That's a nice thought, but I'll come with you.'

Rodney pulled a face, which was supposed to make him look like he was thinking about it. But of course he wasn't thinking about it at all. He had no intention whatsoever of flying around, wearing himself out while lazy Janice stayed home. But as you'll no doubt learn when you grow up and get married, relationship management is largely made up of pretending to do nice things for each other whilst really having ulterior motives. Rodney smiled sweetly at Janice, his yellow teeth gleaming in the light of the bare bedroom light bulb, and went off to do his bathroomy things in the bathroom. Two minutes later he was still there, flossing his teeth with some dog gut, when he heard his darling wife scream his name.

'**Rodneeeeeeeeeeeeeeeeeee!**' screamed Janice, who did tend to overuse vowels when excited. '**Rodderneeeeeeeeee**, come here! Come here now!'

Rodney rolled his eyes. He'd probably left a blister on one of the fingers, and it had worked its way into the smoothie (this was a particular pet hate of Janice's). Or maybe he'd used the wrong glass or something. Still, he thought he'd better go in or she'd throw a sulk and not go out flying that night.

'What is it, my precious?' Rodney said as he walked back into the bedroom.

'Look! Look at this!'

Janice was lying where he'd left her, naked and wrinkly on the floor. But she was holding up to him the *Witch!* magazine, opened to page twelve.

'"Flex your hex for a top Tex-Mex",' he read, squinting at a recipe.

'No, no, below that. Look in the newly developed spells section!'

'"Monpantso Corp. develops new spell for merging animals." So what?'

'So what? So what, he says! So we can merge those cats when we find them. Don't you see? This new merging spell is on the market. All we need to do is to find those pesky cats and I can get my Purrari.'

Janice jumped up, threw the magazine into the corner, and grabbed her cloak and hat. 'Come on,' she said. 'Let's go!'

It was less than twenty minutes later that Rodney and Janice Burringo, evil man-and-wife team extraordinaire, hit the skies. The sun was barely down, and there was still light in the western sky, but out they flew, cackling shadows darker than the night, their eyes so red that if you'd looked up at that moment you would have thought they were the wing lights of a distant plane. Unless of course you'd noticed the broomsticks, the pointy hats, and the cloaks that enveloped them and had run screaming in the opposite direction.

Anyhoo, the Burringos were on form that night. They whooshed and swooshed through the air on their broomsticks, bobbing and weaving, scooting and zooming, ducking and diving, dropping and rising from high-rise to horizon as they scoured the city for the cats. At last, shortly before midnight, Rodney yelled, 'There it is!'

Janice looked up from her position a few hundred metres to the right to see Rodney pointing to the ground below them.

'I don't believe it!' he shouted across to her. 'I thought we'd have to search all night! Look, it's definitely the same taxi.'

'Shush,' said Janice, zooming over to him. 'You're getting overexcited.'

A thin trail of orange gas had started streaming from Rodney's bottom.

'You're right,' he said, pulling himself together and clutching his broomstick more tightly. 'Let's creep down on them.'

Which is what they did. They circled a few times until they were at the right altitude, and then, without a word, they swooped down in a formation known at the Reverse Tornado.

Have I told you what superb flyers Rodney and Janice were? I haven't? Well, Rodney and Janice were superb flyers. They had, in the early days of their romance, been to several flying galas where they had won silver medals in regional championships (Janice's laziness stopping them ever being good enough for gold). Now they put those flying skills to the test. Their Reverse Tornado was so fast, so perfectly executed that within the blink of an eye they were on the taxi, one on each side, arms outspread so that there was absolutely no way anything or anyone inside the vehicle might escape.

'Mwah ha ha ha,' cackled Rodney once he realised the car was now hermetically (look it up) sealed.

'Mwah haa haa haaaa,' echoed Janice. 'We've got you, you furry little pussies. You're toast. You're dead. You're mine. Ha ha haaaaaa!' and a huge trumpet of green gas billowed out the back of her cloak.

A BIT OF A DOG 1

Well, can you imagine how terrifying it would be to be inside that taxi when two horrible foul-smelling but well-trained witches came and hermetically (did you look it up? did you? If you had done, you'd know what it meant now, and wouldn't that feel good, huh?) sealed you in. Imagine their greenish hook-nosed faces squashed against the glass. Imagine the smell from their armpits as they stretched out their arms over the car. Imagine . . .

Actually, don't imagine any of that because it ain't what happened to the cats. Why's that? Because the cats were a good few miles north of the taxi when the Burringos found it. Oh, come on, you thought they were dumb enough to laze around anymore than necessary in a somewhat conspicuous taxi when two angry witches were after them? Well, OK, I'll let you off with half of that. Because truth be told, Tuck was dumb enough.

'I like it here,' he'd said to Ginger over breakfast that morning. They were sitting on the roof of the tiger-striped taxi and enjoying the warmth of the morning sun on their fur. 'The food isn't mushroom sauce, but those mice do taste good.'

'Rats,' said Ginger.

'And just because we haven't found the mushroom

sauce yet doesn't mean we won't find it. The only thing I can't work out is, if we are on the moon, how come when I looked up in the sky last night I could still see the moon up there?'

Now Ginger was faced with a problem. A moral dilemma, you could say. On the one hand, she didn't want to disappoint Tuck too much and tell him they weren't actually on the moon. On the other hand, she was worried that when Tuck did eventually find out he wasn't on the moon he would be so upset he might want to go back to the apartment. Hmm. Tough one. See what I mean?

'It's a reflection,' said Ginger. 'From earth you can see the moon because there's no water in the sky. Here the sky is all water so when you look up you just see a reflection of where you are. Here, have another kidney.'

'Oh. And the mushroom sauce?'

'Well, we'll just have to keep looking for that. It means a bit of a walk though, so you probably won't want to do it.'

'I will!' said Tuck. 'I will if it means mushroom sauce!'

'I don't mean just a short walk. I mean several days' walk. We have to leave the city, cross into the countryside. It'll be at least a week.'

'And you promise we'll find the mushroom sauce?'

'Er . . . sure,' said Ginger, picking her teeth and flicking the bits down to the tarmac. 'As much as you want. You just keep catching rats every night and we'll be fine.'

Now Tuck looked doubtful. He swallowed the last few crumbs of rat's tongue which he'd been saving until last and gave Ginger a long and suspicious look.

They set off straight after breakfast. Ginger knew the Burringos wouldn't fly by day, but she also knew it wouldn't take them long to find the tiger-striped taxi. Even if it hadn't run out of petrol, she would probably have dumped the car and carried on by paw anyway. Being an intelligent and sensible cat, she knew that taxis are easier to spot than cats, no matter how good your eyesight. So all day she and Tuck had walked. It was a bright hot day, the sky the colour of Tuck's sort-of-favourite blue, a day better spent panting in a shadow than traipsing along hot tarmac. But Ginger insisted they push on through the midday heat, the early afternoon heat, the late afternoon . . . Well, you get the idea.

By the time the sky started to fade, and at last a little evening breeze could be felt, the two cats were utterly exhausted. And once more, they were hungry. And you know what happens when you're tired and hungry? Yes, you get grumpy. But more dangerous than that, you start to make mistakes. That's why you should always eat a meal when your parents tell you to, whether you're hungry or not. Skip lunch and next thing you know you might find yourself washed out to sea on a rather large flip-flop which you mistook for a li-lo. Skip dinner and you might wake up in Russia because you got into a train instead of into bed. See the potential peril lurking behind every refusal to consume calories? Well, it was just such a danger that the two cats now walked into.

'Oh,' said Tuck. 'Please can we stop? My paws are killing me.'

Now, Ginger could have pushed him on with a reminder that she'd told him it was going to be a long walk. But she was even more tired than him. After all, Tuck was a streamlined ebony athlete, and she was a flabby middle-aged mog. It was little wonder she replied, 'Yes, I suppose we'd better stop. Next car we come to we'll sit underneath it and maybe settle for the night.'

But they were now in an outer suburb where no cars were parked on the street. They were all locked away in prim little garages or behind painted fences. So the cats walked for another few blocks until eventually, at just about the time Rodney and Janice were swooping down on the taxi, Ginger said, 'This will have to do.' She was wobbly with exhaustion, leaning against a solid wooden fence over the top of which they'd noticed the roof of a large jeep. Tuck helped her squeeze underneath the fence, and then he crept under it himself.

See the mistake? Well, Ginger and Tuck, Tuck and Ginger, our feeble and fatigued feline friends, they looked over the fence, and oh yes, they squeezed under the fence. But oh no, they didn't look *at* the fence. They were so tired, so hungry, so hungry and tired that neither of them took a moment to notice the sign that was hanging there.

Ginger lay under the jeep, exhausted and wondering why she couldn't fall asleep. Something, she knew, was wrong. You see, cats have a sixth sense, which most humans have lost. Not all, but most. This sixth sense is as important to a cat's survival as its ability to feel, smell, taste, see, or hear. It's as intricately woven into the nervous system of a cat—or any animal, come to that—as those five senses, but because we humans have lost it, it is rarely spoken of as anything other than mythical.

The sixth sense is the ability to detect danger. Maybe you have this sense too? Have you ever been in a situation where you knew, without knowing how you knew or why you knew, you just knew something was wrong? And you quickly got out of that situation and only later found out how dangerous it was? You haven't? Don't worry about it.

As I said, most of us don't have this sense anymore. I know I don't. But cats most certainly do, and for all her language skills, cooking ability, and sporting prowess, Ginger was first and foremost a cat. Well, first and foremost a redhead, but second and fivemost she was a cat. And so she opened her eyes and wondered what might be wrong. She turned to look at Tuck, who lay in a heap beside her. He too had his eyes open. He opened his mouth to say something, but Ginger lay her paw on his lips (of course cats have lips!) and frowned deeply. She realised she could hear Tuck snoring. Except there was Tuck awake, which meant maybe it wasn't him snoring after all.

Signalling to Tuck to stay where he was, Ginger dragged her six bellies in a low crawl to the far side of the jeep. Nothing. Just the paved yard and the side fence silent in the light of a streetlamp. Then she belly-dragged to the front of the jeep, the side nearest the house whose garden they had snuck into. There, not one metre from her nose, she saw a large white dog. And not just any white dog. It was a large white pit bull. As I'm sure you're aware, white pit bulls are notoriously nutty and voraciously vicious dogs. It was the pit bull's snoring that Ginger had heard, not Tuck's. A light snuffled snoring from which it would be easy to awake. The dog was nasty-looking, all snout and muscle, no fluffy bits or tail to talk of. Just a lean, mean killing machine. Ginger gulped and started crawling backwards towards Tuck again.

'What is it?' he whispered.

'It's fine. It's just a dog.'

'A DOG!'

Tuck miaowed at the top of his voice and then banged his head on the underside of the jeep as he tried to stand up.

'A DOG! Oh, oh, oh how . . . how . . . a dog!' he yelled. And without a moment's hesitation Tuck scrambled from below the jeep and jumped up onto the fence, balancing precariously on top.

Well, as you can imagine, by the time Tuck had made all this commotion and stood wobbling on top of the fence, there was no more sleeping dog in the yard. There was just a loud, snarling, angry dog. *Bobbo, bobbo, boh*. That was the dog barking, you get it? **BOBBO, BOBBO, BOH! Grrrrr . . . ROH!**

Ginger watched from under the jeep as the pit bull jumped up and barked at Tuck. 'Please let it be chained,' she prayed. 'Please let it be chained up.'

But as she watched the dog's muscular white legs running around the jeep, Ginger could see no chain trailing behind. The dog ran around freely, barking and snarling and sounding more deadly by the minute. Ginger lay perfectly still. Maybe, she thought, maybe the dog wouldn't notice her. She barely dared to breathe as she watched its powerful legs run around the yard. Then they stopped. The pit bull had stopped barking, and Ginger could hear him sniffing the air. Not just the air above him where Tuck was still wobbling somewhere out of Ginger's sight. But the air beside him, beneath him, beneath the jeep.

Suddenly he crouched down and stuck his angry white face under the vehicle, his pink eyes shining brightly, his black nose glinting in the dark. ''Ello there, kitty,' he said, letting his mouth hang open and all his teeth show. Ginger could smell his breath, feel the stinking warmth of it as he snarled his teeth at her. If only she'd followed Tuck like a sheep, making the steep leap from deep below the jeep to the safe-keep of the fence. It made her want to weep. She shut her eyes tightly and prayed it would all be over quickly.

A SMELLY LITTLE BIT

Meanwhile, back at the taxi, can you imagine the scene? Rodney and Janice went from elated to deflated in a very quick minute. They had so convinced themselves that they'd found the cats, got so excited about the opportunity to boil them and skin them alive, so hyper about getting a Purrari . . . well, the comedown was more like a slam-down. It totally took the wind out of their bottoms. It's a strange phenomenon that witches produce gas at both ends of the spectrum of emotions. When they are excited and happy, it's green and orange. When they are quickly deflated, it's invisible but extremely toxic.

'Oh, blast, bother, and blister it!' said Janice, a large tree wilting slowly beside her.

'Gnash, gnash, gnash,' said Rodney, pronouncing the *g* each time so that you have to go back and read it again to get the proper effect. His nose hooked over, and all the warts stuck out, and his face started to turn green. You see, Rodney was more angry than upset. He might have been a male witch, but he was a macho male witch, and he confronted adversity with aggression rather than anything else. He stood there fuming (literally) and thinking hard about what they should do next.

'Why?' wailed Janice. 'Why, why, why must my life be so hard?'

Poor Janice. She was one of those stupid witches who think their lives are hard just because they can't sit around picking their toenails all day. She had no idea she was one of the richest beings in the world. Like you. Oh yes, you. Trust me, if you are reading this book with a roof over your head in a peaceful country with hot and cold running water, you are one of the rich ones. If you don't believe me, try Sudan for the weekend (I'll see you when you've got over the squits). Really, you should try it. Otherwise you might end up like Janice, wailing and crying about her poor miserable life not knowing how good she had it. It's not everyone who can pop down to the shops and pick up a cockroach curry whenever they want to.

'Boo hoo hoo,' she was crying now. '**WOAH wee** wah!'

Janice started banging her head on the roof of the taxi, leaving dull dents in its tiger-stripe paintwork. Rodney ignored her. He'd spotted something inside the taxi that he thought might be important. Can you guess what it was? You guessed it! It was a pale ginger cat hair.

'Aha!' he said, so loudly that Janice stopped her head-banging and looked over the roof of the cab towards him.

'Aha?' she said.

'Aha! Look what I can see!'

He pulled open the door in front of him, reached down to the floor, and picked up the ginger hair.

'Look,' he said (somewhat predictably), 'it's a ginger hair!'

'So?' said Janice. She was sticking out her bottom lip and catching the thick white goo falling from her nose. There were sticky green tears all over her face, and her hair was full of leaves which had fallen off the by-now-completely-dead tree. Rodney thought he'd never seen her looking so beautiful.

'My love,' he said. 'Do you not see? This is all we need. I know any number of good location spells. All we do is combine this hair with the other ingredients, and we'll easily find those miserable moggies.'

Suddenly Rodney could resist no longer. He came around the taxi and gave Janice a long, hard kiss. Then he sucked all the goo out of her nose and swallowed it with a big gulp. 'Oh, how I love you,' he said. 'I'll get you a Purrari, whatever it takes.'

'Oh, Wodney,' said Janice.

'Oh, Janice,' said Rodney.

Now there was no more toxic gas pouring forth from either of them (apart from that stuff that just came out of their mouths), but it was too late for the tree, which was dead right to the tips of its deepest roots. As Rodney and Janice put their broomsticks together so they could straddle them as one and fly off into the black night, the tree first teetered, then it tottered, then with a long, slow creak and a massive great crack it fell over, smack on top of the taxi. Rodney and Janice looked down from their broomsticks, and their horrible cackling filled the night.

'Mwahhahaha! Mwahhahahahaaaaaaaaa…'

A BIT OF THIS, A BIT OF THAT

It wasn't even nearly dawn when the Burringos got back to the apartment, even though they'd been kissing and canoodling all the way back. Rodney logged onto his laptop and went straight onto Spookle, while Janice ran upstairs to slip into something a little more comfortable. I can't tell you what it was because I have no idea what could be more comfortable than a big, baggy witch's cloak, so you'll have to use your imagination. Maybe it was silky undies, who knows. **Anyhoo**, by the time she came back down, Rodney was hard at it, looking for spells.

'Look!' he said. 'There's one here that links into Spookle Maps so you can trace the object of your search as it moves.'

'Rodney . . .'

'But this one's best. It's got hundreds of great reviews on Spellchecker, and the ingredients aren't too bad, and it needs only a tiny percentage of the object. One hair should be fine.'

'Rodney, lover boy, can't that wait? Let's leave it until tomorrow.'

Rodney looked at Janice. 'Don't you want a Purrari?'

'Yes but—'

'Well then. I'm going to make a list of what we

need and go down to the Chelsea drugstore, get my prescription filled at the same time.'

Janice knew when she was beat. Once Rodney Burringo got an idea in his head, there was no stopping him. She'd loved that about him once and indeed had thought it was the reason he was made for money. Now she wasn't so sure. She stomped into the kitchen and flicked on the cauldron to make a cup of pee.

'Have we got any dried buttock?' Rodney called through from the living room.

Janice opened the cupboard and moved some things around to make it sound like she was looking.

'Mmm . . . can't see any,' she said.

This was true. She couldn't see any because although her hand was in the cupboard, her eyes were on a TV listings magazine she'd spotted on the counter. It was open to that night's viewing, and she was scouring for a good soap opera. Shame really, as there was a big unopened tub of dried buttock at the very front of the bottom shelf.

'What about lemons?' said Rodney.

'Mmm?'

'Lemons?'

'Yes, dear,' said Janice, who'd found a fascinating story about the presenter of *Incantation Tonight* and his battle to overcome sympathy. She barely noticed the noise of Rodney getting ready and looking for his keys.

'Right then, I'm off,' he said. 'We need buttocks . . . maybe I can get some fresh . . . and no lemons.'

Janice was halfway back to the living room, a mug of

steaming pee in one hand and the magazine in the other, before she even realised Rodney had gone.

'Oh,' she said. 'He didn't say goodbye. How rude.'

Janice deplored rudeness in any form. It does have its uses though, and for Janice it was an excuse to sulk, open a packet of biscuits and watch the telly with the sound up high. None of which helped her one iota when Rodney arrived home half an hour later with a bag of fresh buttocks and no lemons.

Now, where were we with Ginger and Tuck? Er, something about a fence. Did they go under the fence yet? Oh yes! Tuck was leaping, dog was creeping, Ginger wasn't weeping even though she felt like it. Got it.

With her eyes closed tightly Ginger could clearly hear the dog getting closer and closer. Soon she could feel the warmth of his breath, which smelled, coincidentally, exactly the same as Janice Burringo's favourite perfume, Kennel No. 5. Closer and closer the dog came, so that even the saliva dripping from his fangs could be heard, **slippy sloppy slurp slurp**. But then the dog stopped and said, 'Oh.' Just like that.

''Ere,' he said. 'Ain't you Ginger Jenkins?'

Ginger hadn't been called that in a very long time, and she carefully opened one eye.

'It *is* you!' said the dog, whose huge white fangs were only inches away from her. 'Ginger Jenkins, blow me down. I saw you fight in '37. They showed it again on the telly the other day. You was amazin'.'

'Gulp,' said Ginger. Then she opened her other eye and said, 'Thanks.'

'You not fight no more then?' said the dog. He tilted his head to one side in a way that made him look slightly less terrifying than before. But only slightly.

'Retired,' said Ginger.

'Oh man, you was great in those days. I saw you up against Paw Robeson in the finals. I thought he had you beat. Man, he was a dirty fighter, Robeson. Then you got 'im with your famous five-claw finisher. What you doin' in my yard?'

'Er . . . just needed somewhere to spend the night,' said Ginger. 'That alright?'

'Course not!' said the dog. 'Didn't you see the sign on the fence? It says "Danger—Guard Dog". I start letting cats sleep in 'ere, I'll be a laughing-stock. Won't be able to show my tail down the park without it getting bitten off. Nah, sorry, love, I'm going to have to tear you to pieces.'

'What's your name?' Ginger asked him, blatantly playing for time.

'Brad,' said the pit bull.

'OK, Brad,' said Ginger, thinking quickly. 'How about a fair fight? Just you and me, nose to nose, no gloves.'

'It's not how I normally do it,' said Brad, frowning nastily. He'd turned his head back to normal and was at his scariest again.

'You scared?' said Ginger. 'Worried I'll get the upper paw?'

'Me, scared?' said the dog, backing out from under

the jeep. 'You're on. Come on out here and we'll make a fair fight of it.'

Ginger took a deep breath and followed the dog out into the half-lit yard. He'd already chosen his corner, sitting himself down against the jeep's front tyre.

'You're a big cat,' he said, 'but you're out of shape. You're going to get it, you're going to regret it, you should have taken your chance while you could let it.'

'I hope you fight better than you rap,' said Ginger, who herself could rap faster than a department store shop assistant at Christmastime.

Brad went on undeterred. 'You used to be on telly, now you're just belly, and you know what's worse?' He sniffed the air between them. 'You're even gettin' smelly.'

Ginger rolled her eyes and gave the most gingery sigh in this entire book.

'Brad, that's bad; Brad, that's sad. Rapping fighters was only a fad. You want to get to it? You want to kung fu it? If you have a coach, you'll really want to sue it.'

Ginger's writ-wit was not a hit with the pit. He was champing at the bit, having a fit, couldn't take any more of her showmanship. Then 'Hit it with your mitts,' said Tuck after a bit, thinking he should really do more than just sit.

'Quit it,' said Ginger. 'I'm trying to concentrate.'

But Tuck was excited too now. 'Bite him on his bum, then he'll be glum!' he shouted down from the fence.

'Tuck, please,' said Ginger.

'Who's your friend?' snarled Brad.

'Just someone I brought along to make you look intelligent,' said Ginger. Then she put out one paw and beckoned Brad forward. 'Come on, mutt-face' she said. 'Let's see if you've got any pit to go with all your bull.'

Well, she didn't have to ask twice. The pit bull leapt at her with his mouth wide open, his lips drawn back, and his huge teeth coming full at her. Ginger heard Tuck yowling in fear, but she knew all she had to do was focus. Wait for it, wait for it, and then **slash!** She stuck out all the claws of her left paw and sliced them across the front of the dog's shiny black nose.

Now, as you may or may not know, a dog's nose is possibly the most sensitive part of its body. Imagine how much you'd scream if a cat gave you five deep lacerations on the most sensitive part of your body. Well, that's pretty much how much this dog screamed. And I don't know if you've ever heard a dog yelp for help, but it's a high-pitched and horrible noise. It's so expressive of pain and misery that you can't hear it without wanting to rush to the poor little doggy's assistance. Unless, of course, that poor little doggy has just been trying to kill you, which, I need not point out, was the case here.

Ginger didn't hang around to see if Brad was going to come back for more. She turned on her tail and ran full speed to the fence and squeezed under it and into the street. Tuck saw what she was up to and jumped down beside her, and the two cats ran as fast as they could into the night, leaving the street empty behind them but for the powerful and pitiful, piercing pitches of a pit bull pooch in pain.

It took two hours for Rodney to stop shouting at Janice, get back to the drugstore, find a shop with lemons, and calm himself into a mood for cooking spells. Oh yes, folks, it's all sauce and sorcery in this book. Maybe we should call it that? I know until now it's been called *Cats on the Run*, but from now on we could call it *Sauce and Sorcery*. It has a classic ring to it, don't you think? Oh, suit yourselves.

Eventually, all grew quiet in the Burringos' apartment. Janice had fallen asleep in front of the Occulture Channel, and Rodney had put the TV onto mute. He'd taken his laptop into the kitchen and was switching his attention between the location spell and an old Le Curset cauldron he kept for special spells. He'd mashed up the buttocks in the pestilence and mortar and fried it in some hair oil before throwing in some tongue of frog and eye of newt.

'Fair is foul and foul is fair,' Rodney sang under his breath. 'Hover through the fog and the filthy air.'

This was the difficult part of the recipe. Rodney had to split the cat's hair right down the middle. Now, splitting hairs is a very annoying process and difficult to do when you want to and difficult not to do when you don't. So Rodney laid the ginger hair on the chopping board and focused all his attention on it as he split it straight down the middle. It was a perfect job, the job of a professional, the job of a psychopathic killer (aka witch). He added one half of the hair to the buttock mixture, and then, just as the instructions on the screen of his laptop demanded, he weed into the cauldron for exactly twenty-two seconds.

'Bubble and hiss, boil my peas,' he said, pouring in the 200 grams of frozen peas directed by the recipe. Then he waved his wand airily over the broth and hacked up a really good greeny.

'**Phwar**.' Rodney spat it into the cauldron. 'Cook on the hob, dissolve my gob,' he said, and gave another waft of his wand. Then he turned the heat down to low, set the timer to thirty-four minutes, and went into the living room. He rummaged through the drawers of his desk—not caring a **terwit-terwoo** if he woke Janice up—until he found a map of the city. Back in the kitchen he found the half a hair he hadn't thrown into the cauldron. He carried it carefully back to the map and laid it in the middle.

'Wizardry, witchery, hocus-pocus,' he said, his hand flat above the hair. 'Show me where, let me focus.'

Of course nothing happened because he hadn't drunk the potion yet. What did you think he was doing in the kitchen, steaming his face? This was just a practice to ensure he got it right when he did it for real. For sorcery, like baking, requires great precision. Rodney said the words a few more times until he felt confident he'd got the spell down pat. Then time ticked by slowly in the apartment, and Rodney felt like he was waiting for hours for the spell to be ready.

At last, the timer rang in the kitchen. Rodney ran in, picked up the cauldron, and poured the scorching broth down his throat. It burned of course, but that was part of the spell. Everything has its price, and the price of this spell was first-degree throat burns, which is why there was a hyperlink to first-degree-throat-burns-healing-spells on that page of Spookle.

'**ACHHHH**,' said Rodney, who was not normally as carefree with consonants or vowels as his wife, but it really did hurt. 'Eek.'

Once all the boiling and surprisingly tasty broth was down his throat, Rodney stumbled back to the living room and put his hand flat over the map.

'Xardry, xichkraft, ocush-pocush,' he gurgled through his scorched and blistered lips. 'Xo me ware, let me focush.'

Rodney had no idea if that would be enough. Whoever had written the spell hadn't said how difficult it would be to speak with a loathsomely lacerated larynx. Rodney stood there staring at the map, wondering if his croaking had been sufficient. Maybe nothing would happen. Maybe it would be a waste of time. Maybe he should get to the burns unit. But then a dull blue glimmer appeared above the map, and slowly but surely the split hair began to move.

Rodney steeled himself against the pain in his throat, bits of which were now falling off and going down his gullet. He held himself up on the table and watched the hair as it stood up on one end and moved across the map. Not to the west, east, or south, nor even to the north. No, it headed straight north-east, out past the furthest suburbs and into the countryside. Then it stopped and twirled around a very specific spot. Quickly, Rodney grabbed a pen and drew a circle around that precise point on the map. Then he ran back to the kitchen, yanked open the fridge, and pulled out the bin juice anti-burns potion he'd wisely prepared earlier. 'Ah,' he said as the stinking liquid trickled down his throat. 'How very refreshing.'

Rodney leant against the kitchen counter to catch his breath and panted with relief that the pain had ended at last. Back in the living room he found Janice had woken up.

'What was all that banging and crashing?' she said. '**Pwoar,** it smells of burning throat flesh in here. What have you been up to?'

Rodney told her all about it. She sniffed his breath to check he was telling the truth (and also because she was still feeling a little necromantic from earlier, and there is nothing more attractive to a witch than bin juice on a man's breath).

'Oh, my brave knight,' she said. 'Oh, my big soldier.'

Rodney took Janice's hand and led her over to the table and the map. There, in its top-right corner, was the big red circle he'd drawn not ten minutes before. In it lay the half-hair. Janice watched as Rodney picked it up carefully and placed it into an envelope from the desk drawer.

'Can we use it again?' she said.

'It's good for about a week,' he said. 'We can use it about as often as we want in that time.'

They both peered at the map.

'How did they get so far?' said Janice.

Rodney frowned. 'I don't know,' he said.

'So what do we do now?'

'Now,' said Rodney, watching the sky grow light outside the window and the tired black bags under Janice's red eyes. 'Now we go to bed.'

THIS BIT

The city where this story starts and ends is large and sprawling. Let's face it, most cities are. In the good old days, you had walls around a city, a moat if you were lucky. A clear definition of where the city ended and the countryside began. These days who can tell? Are you in an outer suburb or a separate town? A part of the greater big city or a separate place altogether? Modern life is so difficult. But all urban sprawls run out eventually. Either they hit a coast or a mountain range or—as is the case here—they just stop being so built-up. They have fewer and fewer buildings, let the odd field in, then another and another until, before you know it, you're in the countryside.

'Look!' said Tuck at six o'clock the following morning. 'We're in the countryside.'

Ginger didn't respond. She was trudging along beside him, half asleep. She'd been walking like that for hours. Occasionally she'd fall fully asleep and walk in a weird diagonal that cut across Tuck's path. Then she'd nod suddenly and wake herself up.

'Got to keep going,' she'd say. 'Got to. Keep. Walking.'

But eventually even she had to stop. Actually, I don't know why I say 'even she'. It's not like Ginger is a robust specimen of feline health and resilience, is she? She's a fat ginger cat with six bellies. Now, Tuck, Tuck's a different story. Tuck, could probably have gone on for a while. The point is: Ginger had to stop. The two cats hadn't eaten that night—they had seen no rats for Tuck to play tick with—and they hadn't stopped walking either. So, by the time the sky began to soften and a dull glow appeared in the east, by the time they suddenly found themselves in the countryside, both of them were tired and hungry.

'I have to stop,' said Ginger. 'I need somewhere to sit and rest.'

'What about that big building?' said Tuck.

Ginger's eyes were heavy and half closed, but she still managed to roll them in disdain.

'That's not a building, you moron.' She yawned. 'That's a hedge.'

'No,' said Tuck. 'Look through the hedge. It's a building!'

Ginger squinted through the thick leaves of the hedge beside the road. Tuck was right. A huge old hay barn lay in the field beyond. What a feast for sore eyes!

'Perfect,' she said. 'We'll rest there. And it'll be full of mice, which you can help me catch.'

'You said they were rats,' said Tuck.

'I said they *were* rats and they were. But this is the countryside. We're more likely to see mice now.'

'Why?'

Ginger took a deep breath. She wasn't too tired to pin Tuck to the ground and kick him in the ears.

'Because,' she said, 'on the moon all the rats are terrified of mushroom sauce, so they stay in the cities.

Come on, are we going to this barn or not?'

'What's a barn?' said Tuck.

'It's a kind of spaceship left behind by aliens,' said Ginger over her shoulder as she crawled under the hedge.

Coming out the other side, she found herself in a broad green pasture covered in cowpats. She could see the cows far away on the other side of the pasture, and the sight of them made her feel better. She felt like she was getting closer to home. Then as Tuck crawled under the hedge behind her, asking if the cowpats were made of sauce too and what a barn was again and were they nearly there, Ginger walked across the grass. Well, that made her feel even better. Cats love grass—it relaxes them and puts big fat smiles on their faces.

'Ooh hoo hoo,' said Tuck. 'This green stuff tickles. Ooh, it tastes good too.'

Of course! Ginger had been away so long she had forgotten she could eat grass. She stopped and started nibbling on it, then turned her head to crunch it with her side teeth. 'We'll be seeing this again,' she thought as she ate it, but she carried on regardless. At least it was food. She felt better than she had done in hours. But she knew they should rest, sleep, and eat something they could keep down, so she told Tuck to keep up and walked on to the barn.

Close up it looked even bigger than your average barn. It was a ginormous great building with one side open to the elements.

'What's that stuff?' said Tuck, pointing inside.

'It's hay,' said Ginger. 'It's where the mice live.'

There was plenty of it, huge piles reaching up to the ceiling, tied in bales like giant Lego blocks.

'What's Lego?' said Tuck.

'What?'

'I mean, what's hay?' said Tuck.

'It's dried grass. It's scratchy, warm, and good to lie in.'

'Ooh,' said Tuck. He looked at the great stacks, all of different heights, some only one or two bales tall, some reaching all the way up to the ceiling. Then he took a deep breath and said 'Ooh' again.

The two cats walked in through the great open side of the barn, looking up around them. Have you ever been in a truly huge building? Not one with lots of floors, I mean one with nothing but air between you and the top? Like the Blue Mosque in Istanbul or St Paul's Cathedral in London or Grand Central Station in New York? Other buildings may be bigger, but empty buildings *feel* bigger because you can see further. It's done on purpose in religious buildings to make you feel smaller and more in awe of a bigger power. I'm not sure why it's done with train stations—maybe you can get back to me on that one. In barns it's done so that it's easier to stack hay, but the end effect is all the same: awe.

'Wow,' said Ginger. 'Awesome.'

'I wonder if anyone lives here,' said Tuck.

And then the whole barn echoed to a booming voice, which belonged to neither of them.

'Of course somebody lives here!' it shouted, filling every corner of the cavernous barn. 'I do!'

Now, the more observant of you may have noticed that every time something exciting is about to happen in this story, I whisk you away and start telling you about what was happening on the other side of town. It's a cheap narrative trick, but if you've got this far, it seems to be working. Except now of course I can't do it. Two reasons. Firstly, the cats aren't in town anymore, they're in the countryside. Or 'the bush' as they call it in Australia. I've no idea why Australians call it 'the bush'. It's not like other countries don't have bushes in their countryside. Maybe it's because it's a shorter word? Australians like to abbreviate everything, and 'bush' is as good an abbreviation of 'countryside' as anything else I can think of.

The second reason I can't whisk you away to the other action is because Janice and Rodney are in the secret-upstairs-locked room, snoring away on the floor. Not sure why they're still locking it now the cats are gone, but people are strange and witches are stranger. But whisk you away I will. Not to the contemporary action but to glance at Ginger's history.

You see, I'm thinking you are probably wondering why Ginger was so keen to get back to the countryside-slash-bush. Life at the Burringos' was rather good, after all. A steady supply of food, plenty of soft surfaces to laze the day away on. What could it possibly be that drove Ginger to brave the elevator, risk the wrath of the Burringos, and face starvation and exhaustion on the road? The answer—as is so often the case—is love.

Oh yes. Ginger might have been the original badass-from-the-back-of-maths-class, she might have been as tough as old nails, as sarcastic as a caustic car sticker, as bolshie as a belching butcher from Bendigo, but underneath that Ginger exterior she had a woman's heart. Well, a female cat's heart, but you know what I mean. And even though it was quite far underneath the exterior because of all the bellies and other residual fat, it was a big heart nonetheless. A heart that beat in time to another cat's heart.

I'm not sure anyone really knows how Ginger first met Major 'Mango' Awesome.

It might have been when she was working the clubs in Berlin. (She was a lighting technician; he played triangle in a few of the bands.) Or when she was learning to cook in the South China Sea. Or, I suspect, their paths crossed on the alley-fighting circuit. Either way, from the moment they set eyes on each other, it was fond and feline feeling all the way.

Ginger was a city cat through and through, Major was a country boy, and yet they found they had so much in common. They'd lie on a car roof at night, passing each other stalks of grass and talking about their lives, amazed at how often they'd been in the same place at the same time, passing within a whisker of each other and yet never meeting. Ginger would tell Major of the things she loved and find he was the only cat she'd ever met who knew what she was talking about. Major would express his frustration at the way of the world, and Ginger would say exactly what he needed to hear. He'd finish her sentences, she'd guess what he was thinking about, he'd teach her a new purr he'd heard on the road only to find she knew it too. Ah, love.

Only four weeks after first meeting Major, Ginger thought nothing of hanging up her knuckle-dusters, leaving the city behind, and moving out to the abandoned stables where Major lived, deep in the countryside. And he thought nothing of letting her boss him around, telling him to tidy up and rid himself of his bachelor habits. It was a good life.

But as ever with the good things in our lives, we grow used to them too quickly. Luxuries become necessities, contentment becomes wondering 'what if', comfort becomes boring. Soon both Ginger and Major remembered that they had once been ambitious for more. They both missed their lives on the road. 'Let's save up,' said Ginger. 'Let's buy a one-way ticket to somewhere and see what happens next.' And so they'd started driving the taxi, taking turns so when one of them was sleeping, the other was driving. It meant commuting to the city and seeing each other less often, but they both figured it would be worth it in the end.

Well, this little living arrangement was all going fine and dandy until one night Major and Ginger had a terrible fight. It was about nothing—all the big fights are—and it was about everything. Have you ever heard adults argue? Awful, ain't it? But it's part of life, part of living together, and cats are no different.

On the night in question, Ginger and Major had a real humdinger. They ended up on the stable floor, doing that low whiney moan which cats do when they are seriously unimpressed. **Nnnngggggeeeeeuuuuugggghhhh**. Then Ginger said, 'Eat my litter', and walked out in a big huff. She threw her possessions into the boot of the cab and drove off. Of course as soon as she reached the city she realised what a mistake she'd made. She tried calling Major from a call box but then remembered there was no phone at the stables. So she turned the cab around and started driving back to say sorry, to say they should work it out. To tell Major how much she loved him and how much she wanted to be with him forever. Just then she saw a nice-looking man on the sidewalk, looking for a cab. 'Oh well,' thought Ginger. 'I'll just do this fare and then I'll drive home.'

Except of course that nice-looking man was not nice at all. He was not a man at all—he was evil Rodney Burringo, the kidnapping old buzzard. And the rest, as they say, is this story. Or the bit before this story and then this story if you want to split hairs about it (which I know you don't). Poor Ginger! She had no way of letting Major know she hadn't left him. No way of telling him she'd never do that. All she wanted to do was get back to him as fast as she could.

Meanwhile back in the barn . . . Oh no, not meanwhile at all. Actually, it's four and a bit years later back in the barn. Ha, and you thought you were sharp. So, back in the barn . . .

'I wonder if anyone lives here,' said Tuck.

And then the whole barn echoed to a booming voice, which belonged to neither of them.

'Of course somebody lives here!' it shouted etc. 'I do!'

Ginger spun around in an instant, tail puffed up and claws at the ready. Tuck couldn't even do that. He was entirely frozen to the spot in panic. It was just like the most frightening scene from his least favourite horror movie when Dorothy and her friends go to see the wizard for the first time.

'Who,' said the booming voice, 'are you?'

Tuck was shaking so hard he could hardly stand. If he wasn't such a well brought-up cat, he'd have wet himself there and then. Ginger came over and stood next to him, pressing against him to stop him shaking.

'We,' she said, 'are two cats who are not afraid to show our faces. What about you?'

'No,' Tuck whispered to her. 'Don't upset the mighty wizard! He might do that thing with the green smoke.'

But Ginger coughed a little and let out a huge yowl. 'Out! Come on out, you coward.'

'I am out,' said the booming voice. 'Up here.'

Now Tuck turned, leaning on Ginger as if she was the back of a sofa. The two of them looked up to a rickety wooden ledge high above the open entrance to the barn. There sat a row of six cats looking down at them. There was a lean black cat with white patches and a muscular tortoiseshell cat with weird eyes. There were two hugely fat tabbies, who were obviously father and son, and a beautiful Siamese. And the last cat—much to the horror of Tuck (and Ginger, except she didn't admit it)—the last was pure white. Yikes! There is little more dangerous in life than a pure white cat. They scratch, man, they scratch bad. Next to the white cat, who was actually the smallest of the six, was a metal stand that held the biggest megaphone you've ever seen in your life. Well, if you'd seen it, it would be the biggest, but this will have to be the biggest megaphone anyone's ever described to you. Huge, really. As Ginger and Tuck watched, the mean, evil, scratchy-looking white cat leaned towards it.

'Now,' she boomed. 'Who are you?'

Tuck gasped in horror as Ginger burst out laughing.

'A megaphone!' she said, chortling away and making Tuck bump alongside her as she shook with the laughter. 'A megaphone! If you had any self-respect, you'd come down here and speak to us cat-to-cat. Or at least shout down. Ha! A megaphone she needs!'

'Ssh!' said Tuck. 'Don't upset her. She's white.'

But it was too late. The little white cat looked very upset, and the other five cats looked upset about her being upset. Well, four of them did. The Siamese just sat there and looked beautiful—you know what they're like.

'Oh,' said Tuck. 'Oh, maybe we should go? Maybe we should just move slowly to the exit, and they'll forget we were ever here.'

'Tuck,' said Ginger, 'if you move so much as a muscle before I tell you to, I'll bite you so hard that I'll have to go to the litter tray to get rid of the fur ball. Do you understand?'

She said it with a fixed smile on her face and in a voice Tuck had never heard her use before. He sat down and nodded slowly. High above them the little white cat had walked to the edge of the ledge. She was yelling something down to them, but all they could hear was a faint squeak, which might have been from one of the swallows that was flying between the rafters.

'Sorry,' said Ginger. 'I can't hear you.'

The white cat tried again. She seemed to be trying with all her might, her eyes squeezed shut and her tail waving in the air behind her. From the corner of her eye Ginger could see Tuck had stood again and was moving around strangely, but she ignored him and stared up to the ledge.

'Can't hear you,' said Ginger. 'What?'

So the little white cat went back to the megaphone and leant in towards it.

'I had throat cancer last year,' she boomed. 'I had an operation, and now I can make myself heard only through a megaphone.'

'Ooh,' said Tuck, nudging Ginger in the side. 'That's embarrassing.'

'Rubbish,' said Ginger quietly. 'It's not embarrassing at all. She's probably making it up.'

'Why are you blushing then?'

'I never blush!' hissed Ginger under her breath.

'Well, that's weird because you're blushing now!'

Hang on a second, I can hear you thinking. Hang on, hang on, hang on. Wasn't Tuck only two minutes ago quaking in his paw pads? Where has all this cheekiness come from? Oh, go on then, I'll tell you anyway. It was the slinky Siamese up on the ledge. While the white cat had been trying to make herself heard using just her voice, the Siamese had smiled at Tuck. Then she'd winked at him. Then she'd slowly licked one paw and, all the while holding eye contact with him, wiped it across her ear. Hoochie handbags! Well, Tuck forgot all his fear at once and started waving back like a madman until Ginger's embarrassment distracted him.

'Ha ha,' said Tuck. 'You're embarrassed.'

Ginger ignored him. 'Why are you all up there?' she shouted up to the ledge.

It was the flabby tabby daddy who answered. 'We can't come down there' he said. 'There's rats.'

Tuck looked at Ginger smugly, but she ignored him.

'Huge rats,' said the tortoiseshell, scouring the floor with his weird eye. 'They bite.'

'Rats?' said Ginger. 'Rats are food! How can they be frightening?'

The white cat leant into the megaphone again. 'We don't eat meat in this commune,' she boomed. 'We don't believe in hurting other living beings.'

'Right,' said Ginger. 'So what do you eat?'

'They give us dried food up at the house,' said the flabby tabby babby. 'It's yummy and stops our poo from smelling.'

After that, none of the other cats could think of what to say.

A BIT WITH A BAZOOKA

Half an hour later Tuck and Ginger were high up on the ledge with the barn cats. The black-and-white cat had introduced himself as Harry and invited them up. 'All are welcome here,' he said. 'You have nothing to fear.' So up and up the bales of hay Ginger and Tuck had climbed. Ginger was fearless of course but slow, stopping on every bale to drag her bellies up after her. Tuck could get from one bale to another in one easy spring, but after only four or five bales, he started whimpering at how high up he was.

'Don't look down,' said Ginger. 'Concentrate on helping me instead.'

'But . . .

'No buts,' said Ginger. 'Here, see if you can drag this last belly up for me.'

Well, helping with six bellies is difficult when you can't count past three, and before Tuck knew it they were at the top. The first thing Ginger did was quietly and quickly apologise to the little white cat for her insensitive comments. The little cat shrugged and said something in reply, which Ginger couldn't quite make out. Rather than ask the white cat to repeat herself, Ginger walked over to the others and introduced herself.

'I'm Ginger,' she said, 'and this is—'

'Tuck! Hi! I'm Tuck, hi, everyone,' said Tuck, jumping around excitedly. 'My name's Tuck. Hello, hello.'

The flabby tabbies introduced themselves as Barry and his son, Larry. They were from Gary, Indiana.

'Hi, Larry! Hi, Barry!' said Tuck, rushing towards them.

'I'm Carrie,' said the white cat into the megaphone.

'Hi, Carrie!' said Tuck, running back that way.

'I'm Ari,' said the tortoiseshell with the weird eye.

'Hi, Ari,' said Tuck, turning to run again.

'Hi,' said the Siamese. 'I'm Sally. What's your name?'

'Hi, Sally!' said Tuck. 'I'm . . . agggghhh!'

The six cats from the barn thought this was a very strange name, but Ginger knew something was wrong. She'd been sniffing Harry's nose to see what dried food smelled like, but now she whipped round in time to see Tuck teetering on the rim of the ledge, nothing between him and the ground twenty metres below. He'd been running back and forth so excitedly he'd not noticed himself getting closer and closer to the edge. Ginger strolled over and grabbed him by the scruff of his neck and dragged him back towards the other cats.

'This is Tuck,' she said. And then she took a step back so Tuck couldn't see her as she mouthed 'raised in a cage' to the others. They all smiled at Tuck sympathetically. All apart from Sally, who walked up and started licking his face.

'Ooh,' said Tuck. 'Tickles.'

Well, as you can imagine, the cats in the barn had a hundred questions for the cats on the run, and the cats on the run had a hundred questions for the cats in the barn. Each. Why they chose to live in a commune, how big were the rats, who won the Eurovision. On and on they went, talking through the morning. Tuck asked ninety-nine of his questions about mushroom sauce; Ginger mostly asked for directions. Harry, the black-and-white cat, took her up into the rafters and along to a high window in the pointiest pointy end of the barn's front wall. He pointed out some distant hills and a line of motorway that appeared now and again in the forest before them.

'That way's north-east,' Harry said. 'But if you go that way on paw, you'll have to cross the Great Dark Forest. Maybe you should go back to town and get a ride?'

'Not an option,' said Ginger, squinting through the window to the hills in the distance. 'Thanks though.'

Harry shrugged and sensing Ginger needed some time alone, he said he'd see her back down on the ledge. Knowing when to leave someone alone is one of the greatest skills in life. Like knowing when to stop talking or when to run away and say a big boy did it, it is an indispensable life skill, which I recommend you start learning right now. **Bendyway**, Harry picked his way back down to the ledge and listened to Sally try to explain to Tuck what mushroom sauce was made of.

'Sauce,' she said, 'and mushrooms.'

Meanwhile, Ginger stayed in the high window and surveyed the land below. The hills Harry had pointed out seemed a long, long way away, and the Great Dark Forest this side of them looked great and dark. But she looked carefully on until her eyes grew heavy, and she found she was wobbling slightly on the narrow window ledge. She remembered she hadn't slept at all the night before. In the excitement of finding the barn she'd forgotten her tiredness, but now it had caught up with her. So she picked her way down through the rafters and found the other cats on the ledge, all lying silently, apart from Tuck, who was sprawled out in the middle of them, mumbling slightly in his sleep. Ginger made out the words 'rush' and 'moom' before she too fell into a deep and dreamless slumber.

It was an hour and a half and a bit after dark when Rodney and Janice began to stir. They'd been through an emotional roller coaster over the previous days, and it had exhausted them more than a real one would have done. The pain of losing their cats, the joy at thinking they'd found them again, the excitement at realising . . . Oh well, look, you've been reading the blooming book, you've got the idea. They'd been up and down like a manic madman on a pogo stick on a trampoline during an earthquake after drinking too much coffee. It was no wonder they had a bit of a lie-in. But eventually they were dozing rather than really sleeping, and the memories of what had happened that morning started creeping in.

'Location spell,' said Rodney, suddenly sitting up. 'We've got a location spell—we can find those fleeing felines. Janice, **boogly-doops**, wake up, my sweet **munchelbag**.'

'Oh, Wodney,' said Janice in her baby voice without opening her eyes. 'Janice is berry, berry tired and wants to sleep a teensy-weensy bit more. Can I have just ten more minutes?'

Well, as you will have noticed if you're a get-up-and-go kind of person, when a lazy person says 'just another ten minutes', it never means just another ten minutes. It means 'when I feel like it'. So Rodney got up and showered, shaved, and moisturised, and left Janice asleep. At first he was a bit annoyed, thinking how he'd gone and boiled his innards and yet his slovenly covenly witch of a wife couldn't even drag her sorry bones out of bed. But then—as he dabbed his Men's Hexpert Wrinkle Remover onto his cheeks—he realised that without Janice slowing him down he could get to the cats even quicker. He had a map, he had his boy-racer broomstick with go-faster stripes, and he could zoom through the sky like the young witch he used to be. Anyone seeing him would think of him as young, free, and evil. Rodney chose a particularly tight-fitting cloak and dressed in a speedy silence so he could claim to Janice later on that she'd simply not woken up in time.

Out in the night sky Rodney felt like a new witch. Of course, most of his throat was new, but Rodney felt like he'd had his whole body replaced. He felt younger and fitter than he had in years. 'It's the challenge,' he said to himself. 'It's the idea of possibility.' He flew a loop-the-loop and gave a whoop to test his newfound **ballyhoop**. 'Oh yes, folks!' he cried. 'Rodney Burringo is back.'

Then he consulted his map and gave an extra strong fart so that he shot across the sky far faster than the speed limit. And who could blame him? It was a beautiful night for flying, the first real night of winter with great white clouds sailing across the inky sky, blowing from horizon to horizon and suggesting travel to distant places full of romance and without the inconvenience of modern airports. It was windy high in the sky, but for Rodney the wind was behind him (in more ways than one), and he sped along towards his destination like a... like a... well, like a farty witch chasing after a cat, I suppose.

The place marked on the map was a long way out of town, but Rodney had been in the Boy Sprouts, and he knew how to read the lay of the land. He followed ridgelines and valleys, ley lines and gulleys, power cables and fire tracks and fences and trolleys. OK, not trolleys but, hey, poetic licence, never heard of it? What?! You've never heard of poetic licence? Oh, it's great! You'll love it! It's basically lying, but you're allowed to do it.

Anyhoo, within no more than two hours, Rodney was hovering in a circle exactly above the place the half-a-hair had pointed to on the map. 'Mwah ha,' thought Rodney, feeling very young and very evil. 'Mwah ha ha ha.' Then he caught himself celebrating too early like bad baddies always do and stopped. 'Focus,' he told himself. 'Act like a professional.'

Rodney approached the farm buildings in slow circles before landing on the roof of the largest of them with the soft tread of a seasoned spooker. Then, after confirming there was no one in sight, he flew down to the ground. Around him several old farm buildings formed three sides of an empty farmyard. The largest was an empty milking shed, half collapsed, one side open to the elements. Opposite it were some stables in a long, low building with a doorway at each end. And at the end of the courtyard were the remains of a house in an even worse state of disrepair than the shed.

Rodney pricked up his ears to see what he could hear, but there was nothing. All was still. If you or I had been there, we'd have thought, 'Let's get the hell out of here and find somewhere more fun instead' because we'd have thought it was completely abandoned. But Rodney didn't think this at all. Oh pepperoni no. Rodney could smell cat. He tipped his head back, flared his nostrils, and took in a big deep breath of air through his warty, yellow nose. 'Mmm,' he said. 'Ginger cat—I'd recognise that pong anywhere.' He couldn't smell a black cat, but that didn't bother him. One cat would lead him to the other. And worse come to worst, he could always find another black cat. It was the smart ginger one that was the key to the experiment.

Rodney leaned his broomstick against the side of the milking shed and started walking towards the stables. Suddenly he was blinded by a horribly bright light. It was directed straight at him from the roof of the stables. Now, if you've been paying attention you may have noticed witches are not fond of light. In fact, they *hate* it. There are some witches who are actually afraid of the light in the same way that you and I are afraid of the dark. Yes, you are. Well, Rodney wasn't normally one of these, but, ouch, that light hurt. He could feel it undoing all the benefits of his very hexpensive moisturiser. He put up one clawed hand to shield his eyes and used the other to cast a particularly nasty spell in the direction of the floodlight. The spell made it no more than a metre before bursting like a particularly pus-filled zit and splattering all over the ground. That's why witches hate light, you see; it weakens their evil powers.

'Dude, can I help you there?' said a voice up behind the giant bulb.

'Er...' said Rodney. 'Er... you could turn off the light.'

'Who are you?'

'My name's Rodney and I'm... er... I'm lost. Who are you?'

'My name, dude, is Mind Your Own Business,' said the voice behind the light. 'You're a witch. What are you doing here?'

Now, Rodney was blinded by the light and feeling weak and awful, but he still had a good brain in his head. He knew that a little bit of truth always improves a lie, so he said, 'I've lost my cat.'

'Oh yes?' said the voice. 'What was the name of this cat?'

'Er . . . Ginger.'

There was silence for a while. Then the light swung slightly away from Rodney, allowing him to stand and stop shielding his eyes.

'How long have you had this cat?' said the voice.

'Four years,' said Rodney.

'And how did you get it?' said the voice.

Now, I don't know about you, but I hate it when people keep asking questions. Any more than three questions in a row is a bit rude, if you ask me. You might want to watch out for that next time you're interrogating your parents. **Bennyway**, Rodney was pretty ticked off by now. What was this, interview cabaret?

Well, if there's one thing that reinvigorates a witch's powers, it's a temper. Rodney lifted his clawed finger again, took a deep and angry breath, and threw another spell at the floodlight, which was now casting its light on the remains of the farmhouse. *KEPOW!* It exploded darkness into the night, tiny fragments of glass shooting in all directions and bouncing off Rodney's leathery face. He heard what sounded like a miaow of surprise and looked up at the roof of the stables, where the light had been operated from, in time to see the end of a ginger tail jumping down behind the roof. He grabbed his broomstick and raced up there to find not Ginger, but a paler ginger cat running along the guttering behind the roof.

Rodney raised his claw again and—full of strength now—let go a lightning bolt at this cat. *KAZOOM!* It missed—hey, you try shooting a lightning bolt at a running redhead and see how well you go—and instead blew a huge hole in the roof of the stables. When the smoke from this had cleared, the cat was nowhere to be seen. Rodney thought carefully for a second and then flew his broomstick in through the hole he'd just blown in the roof.

He found himself in a long, dark, empty space, so long unused it didn't even smell of horses anymore. He cruised slowly above the stalls, dipping his head to stop it hitting on the beams that crossed the roof space. 'Here, kitty, kitty,' he called. 'Come to daddykins.'

But the cat was obviously too smart to listen to an invitation from a witch. Have you worked out who that cat was yet? Oh, come on, what do you want, a diagram? It was Major, of course, Ginger's long-lost lover boy. The best percussionist since Oliver the Octopus, the one-man octet. The hair which Rodney had picked up in the taxi was Major's, not Ginger's. Ginger was still miles away, trying to get back to these stables, trying to get away from the witches to the exact spot where Rodney Burringo was. Do I have to point out the irony of that? Do I? Really? Oh, OK. It was really ironic. Like crazy ironic. If you'd been there, you'd have said, 'OMG, isn't this like **soooo** ironic!' And you'd have been right.

Now then, at this point in the story there is something I need to tell you about Major 'Mango' Awesome. You see, being an older male meant that Major could be a little bit moody. Not all the time, I need to stress, in fact not much of the time. Most of the time he was cool, man, he was a dude, he was a seriously laid-back puddycat. Do you know what 'supine' means? It means lying down. So, if you think about it, being really laid-back, Major was a supine feline. Get it? Yeah? No? Oh suit yourself.

Anyhoo, the reason Major and Ginger got on so well was that whereas she was quite sarcastic and impatient, Major was very easy-going. His favourite thing to do all day was nothing. His favourite food was whatever you gave him. His favourite topic of conversation was silence. He was chilled. But of course this was only most of the time. He was, after all, only feline, and like anyone else Major could be a complete and utter grump. Ginger used to call him a Grumpy Lugger or a Lumpy Grugger, or when she was really annoyed, a Bumpy Grugger. And most of the time he didn't mind because he was too dudey to care. But sometimes he did, and that was when he had a major grump on.

When Major got a big grump on, you really knew about it. Like now, for example, when a witch had turned up outside his stables after midnight on a Thursday and had blown a hole in his roof. Oh boy, that seriously grumped him out. Fortunately though, Major was prepared for such annoyances. Hence the spotlight. And hence too (the sequel) the rocket launcher he kept stored under his bed. Rodney was right that Major had run into the barn, but he was **wrongedy wrongedy ding dang dongedy** if he thought Major was going to come out unarmed. As Rodney hovered over the last stall in the stable, he heard a voice behind him.

'Hey, wart-face,' it said. 'Call *this* back to daddykins.'

Rodney turned to see Major standing on his hind legs, propping up the front of the rocket launcher. He yelled, 'Noooo!' in a deep slow-motion voice just as Major pressed the big red Shoot Rocket button on the side of the weapon. *BOWAKA!* There was a huge boom as the rocket shot out of the launcher and towards Rodney, who barely had time to duck before it shot over his head.

Now Major, being ginger, was a smart cat, but unfortunately, he had slightly miscalculated the aerodynamic, thermodynamic, vectordynamic dynamics, and as the rocket passed over Rodney's head, it zoomed straight through the wall of the stables and landed in the ruins of the farmhouse.

There it made a huge explosion, all red and yellow and flaming like in a really good action movie, where people walk away in slow motion without looking back.

KABOOM! (Then **rackety rackety rackety** as all the bricks and bits of wood fell smouldering to the ground.)

Now, as stated, Rodney had ducked so he was safe. But, oopsa-daisy, what did he find when he sat up again? He found he had a huge rocket-size hole in his witch's hat. Oh dear. Now, you know full well that witches get stronger when they get angry. But did you know you should never ever mess with a witch's hat? You didn't? How have you survived this long? Listen to me: you should never, ever mess with a witch's hat. Not even those yellow plastic ones they use for marking out road works. Oh bells no. There's many a young man or woman who has thought it funny to steal one of those on the way home from the pub. But where are those young men and women now, eh? Where indeed. Old and wrinkly and horrible, that's where. That's what happens to you when you mess with a witch's hat. So now Rodney was ef-you-are-eye-oh-you-es **FURIOUS**!

'Wah!' he roared, his face turning fully green and his nose hooking so far over it tickled his chin. '**Wah-ah-agggh**!' with all the g's pronounced.

Rodney flew down the stables, the wind flapping at the hole in his hat, in the direction he'd last seen Major. There he found another hole in the wall, a hole the shape and size of a cat holding a rocket launcher. He laughed as he realised what had happened. Major had completely forgotten to take the recoil from the rocket into account. Just as it had forced the rocket out towards Rodney, so it had shot Major and itself back through the rotten old wall of the stables. Rodney dismounted and picked his way through smoking broken scraps of wood. In the middle of them he found the rocket launcher, and under the rocket launcher he found Major lying very still. Rodney bent down and pressed his fingers against Major's neck. There was still a pulse.

'Mwah ha ha,' cackled Rodney. 'Mwah ha' etc.

He picked Major up by the scruff of his neck (the cat version of the Vulcan stun grip) and carried him back to his broom. Then he soared away from the smoking stables, the exploded remains of the house, the darkened milk shed. It all looked so peaceful and quiet down there that just for extra evilness Rodney dropped a fireball onto the scene. It hit the ground and exploded, setting all the farm buildings on fire. '**Mwah ha ha,**' he cackled. '**Mwe he he.**' Then he swooped even higher into the sky, all the time with Major held tightly against his chest. 'Who needs Ginger?' Rodney thought. 'I've got the perfect replacement!'

And he raced home to show Janice what he had found.

THAT BIT

Ginger woke suddenly. She lay for a moment or two, trying to remember where she was. Oh, how she loved that feeling. It was the feeling of freedom. For four long years she'd woken up every morning, every afternoon, every evening, and every night knowing exactly where she was. You see, when you sleep as often as a cat does, you wake up pretty often too.

Anyhoo, Ginger woke suddenly. She could hear Tuck sleeping beside her, snoring in his typically annoying way, just too quietly for her to be able to complain about it but just loud enough to be disturbing. Normally this drove her nuts, but tonight she just listened, then smiled as she heard him start talking in his sleep. 'Ooh, yes, please,' he said. 'Ooh, yes, I do agree, I think so, ever so much.'

Ginger stood up and arched her back. It had grown dark while she'd been sleeping, and apart from Tuck's snores and sleepy mumbles, the barn was silent. There was no sign of any of the other cats—who had presumably gone up to the house for their dinner—and Ginger wondered why she'd woken up. She listened to her bellies one by one, but they were no more hungry than normal. She was wondering if maybe she needed to go to the toilet (no more litter trays—hoorah!), but no, all seemed calm in that department too. Then she heard a noise up above her.

'Ooh,' it went. And then, 'Aah.'

She looked up and saw the barn cats hadn't gone for dinner at all. They were sitting next to one another inside the high window where Harry had shown her the way to the hills. They were looking at something going on outside. Well, Ginger didn't want to wake Tuck so instead of shouting to the cats, she carefully made her way up through the rafters. Harry was the first to spot her, and he signalled for her to approach.

'What is it?' Ginger said. 'What are you looking at?'

'Look,' said Harry. 'Over in the hills where you were asking about today. Something is going on.'

Ginger looked and saw in the distance, right where she'd told Harry she wanted to go, a bunch of orange flames tickling the sky.

'There were some explosions,' said Harry. 'We came running up but they'd finished. Now it just looks like the whole place is on fire.'

Ginger didn't respond. She just sat there with her mouth open, staring at the distant flames.

'What's out there?' said Harry, seeing the expression on her face.

'I don't know,' said Ginger. 'There used to be this beautiful old farm. But maybe something else has been built in the meantime.'

She didn't sound very convinced, and Harry didn't question her any further. They just sat there in silence, looking at the flames with the other cats until they heard

Tuck yowling below them.

'**Waaa-ow**,' he yowled. 'I fell asleep, and everyone left me, and it's dark, and I'm scared. Monsters are going to get me, and no one cares because I'm just a lonely orphan. Waaa-ow. I fell asleep . . .'

But by the time he'd yowled all this, Ginger and the barn cats (top name for a pop group!) had run down and were comforting him.

'We're here,' said Sally, touching him nose to nose. 'It's OK.'

'Oh,' said Tuck. 'That's a relief. What's for dinner?'

The barn cats all looked a bit embarrassed by this, and none of them said anything until Harry coughed.

'Er,' he said. 'We all went up to the farmhouse for our biscuits whilst you were asleep. We meant to bring you some back, but we didn't.'

'Sorry,' said the flabby tabby babby, who looked particularly guilty. 'It's just we had no way of carrying them.'

'That's right,' said his daddy tabby, which somehow made the excuse sound even less convincing.

Tuck's bottom lip started quivering, and he looked like he might start yowling again until Ginger put a calming paw on his back and said, 'Don't worry, everyone. We catch our own dinner. Don't we, Tuck?'

'Do we?' said Tuck. 'What are we having?'

'Well, I was thinking maybe a tasty rat-goo,' said Ginger with a silent *t*.

'Ooh,' said Tuck. 'When will it be ready?'

'I tell you what, Tuck. You go downstairs and play chase me with all the little animals there, and as soon as you get back, we'll start cooking. How does that sound?'

Tuck didn't even answer. He just ran to the edge of the ledge and jumped onto the tallest stack of hay, ignoring the strange look Ari gave him and Larry's cry of 'Be careful, they bite!' Then he jumped **boing boing boing** down the bales until he was at the bottom.

Well, can you imagine the scene down there when the rats started to come out? Tough, you're going to have to. This is a book after all, not a video game. Easier on the thumbs, but it does require a bit of an effort. Here, I'll help. It was very, very dark at the bottom of the barn. The big opening in its side faced east, where the sky was at its very darkest that night, and the fire in the distant hills made no dint in the gloom.

Now, as you know, cats can see in the dark. Not in the pitch-black, of course. Then they're as blind as we are. But as long as there's a tiny bit of light they can use that to guide them. And although it was very, very dark on the floor of the barn, there was just enough light from the stars in the night sky coming through the open side of the barn for Tuck to see perfectly clearly. At first he sat still, wondering if maybe Ginger had tricked him and there weren't any animals down here after all. He was still a little sleepy from having just woken up, so he decided to close his eyes and count to ten. If there was no one to play with when he opened his eyes again, he'd go back up to the ledge. So he closed his eyes and of course immediately became completely invisible. Black cat, dark barn, deep shadows—even he'd have had difficulty seeing himself.

The rats had no chance. Thinking no one else was about, they came scurrying out to see what they could find to leave icky germs on. Then Tuck opened his eyes again. Wow! He couldn't believe it! Ginger hadn't been joking at all—there were lots and lots of animals to play with.

'Ooh,' Tuck said. 'Dodgeball! Let's play dodgeball! We've no ball but **grrramp**,' and he bit the closest rat in the back of the neck. 'Got you!' he said. 'My turn, my turn!' Well, as you can imagine, in the space of four minutes none of the rats was playing anything but harps. 'Oh,' said Tuck. 'That's boring.' And he climbed back up to the ledge to find the six barn cats staring at him with open mouths and Ginger blending some garlic into a block of butter.

'That was amazing,' said Sally.

'That was inspirational,' said Harry.

'That was appetizing,' said the two tabbies together.

Then they all gathered around him and asked him how he'd done it. They made him flex his muscles and show them his teeth.

'Break it up, break it up,' said Ginger from the corner where she was dropping pinches of saffron into a steaming pot. 'Tuck, bet you can't run down and bring up all those dead rats in under a minute. Go!'

Well, if the barn cats had been impressed before, now they were blown over. Tuck went down and up, up and down, six times from the high ledge to the distant barn floor. Each time he came up he was dragging a big dead rat in his mouth. Each time he went down he was so fast he was just a blur in the shadows.

'How did I do?' he said when he'd plonked the last rat down in front of Ginger.

'Fifty-three seconds,' she said, dusting flour off her bellies. 'Not bad. Now go and wash your paws and see how many of your fans want to join us for dinner.'

The answer was six, and those six pussycats were half an hour later all turning their compliments from Tuck to Ginger as they wolfed down their delicious second dinner.

'What a wonderful cook you are,' said Barry.

'Marvellous,' said Larry.

'Great,' said Ari, looking at Ginger strangely.

Harry said nothing. He just purred as he ate and looked at Ginger with soft eyes. Now, I don't know if you know this or not, but unlike humans, cats prefer their second dinner to their first dinner. That's why they always yowl for more food even when you've already fed them. In fact, the only thing they prefer to a second dinner is a third breakfast. Of course, they never eat lunch.

'We're so happy to have you here,' said Sally, who was sitting half on the floor and half on Tuck's lap. 'Will you stay forever?'

'No,' said Ginger in a sad but firm tone. 'No, we have to leave in the morning.'

'In the morning?' said Tuck forlornly. 'But we only just got here. And it's warm, and there's lots of animals to play with, and the food's great, and . . . and . . .'

The six barn cats looked at Ginger, and they all said 'Please stay' in a way which would tug on the cat gut of almost any cat in the world. But not Ginger. She had seen fire over her home, and she knew she had to go.

'Let Tuck and me talk about it in private,' she said. 'Then we'll see.'

Well, we all know what 'We'll see' means. It means either 'no' if it's from a strict or unreliable person or 'yes' if it's from a softie. And none of the barn cats could believe that anyone who could cook as well as Ginger could be anything but a softie at heart. How wrong can you be?

Still, Ginger let them think what they wanted. She didn't want to spoil their enjoyment of what until now had been a wonderful night. She left them chatting and deconstructing, for the fiftieth time, Tuck's catching of the rats and her own cooking of them, and picked her way carefully up through the rafters to the window. The fire in the distant hills had dulled to no more than a few wisps of grey smoke. Ginger heard Tuck coming up behind her—he couldn't even walk quietly, that cat— and waited for him to speak first.

'Why do we have to talk about it in private?' he said. 'Why can't we stay?'

'You can stay,' said Ginger. 'I can't tell you what you can and can't do. But I can't. I have to get back to my home—if I've still got a home left.'

And then, without prompting, she told him all about Major and their fight and her kidnapping and the farm beyond the Great Dark Forest. Tuck had never heard her speak so much in all the four-and-a-half years he'd known her. And he'd never, ever thought he might see her cry. And he was right, he would never see that, but as Ginger spoke he started crying for her.

'That's awful,' he said.

'But you like it here,' said Ginger. 'You can stay. And Sally likes you—you're a real local hero.'

'Actually,' said Tuck, 'Sally's a bit annoying, and her bottom smells funny. But I do like it here. I think I would like to stay.'

Ginger nodded and looked back through the window. 'That's fine,' she said. 'Just do me a favour. Don't make a fuss when I leave. I hate goodbyes. I'd rather just sneak away.'

'When are you going?'

'As soon as everyone's asleep. Look at them.'

Tuck followed her gaze down and saw the six barn cats curled up across various parts of the ledge, like six cat-coloured circles. They looked like they were already asleep.

'That's now then,' said Tuck.

'That's right,' said Ginger. 'This is goodbye.'

Tuck started crying again, so Ginger pressed her nose to his. Then she brushed past him and made her way back down through the rafters to the ledge. Tuck watched as she picked her way between the sleeping cats, across to the edge of the ledge and onto the highest stack of hay. She jumped down each stack in turn, much more easily than she'd climbed them, until she reached the barn floor. Then she looked up and there, at the very highest point of the barn, she could see Tuck waving sadly at her, a tiny silhouette against the starlit window. She gave him a little wave in return, and then turned and left the barn.

WHABOUT ABOUT ANOTHER BIT?

Meanwhile, back at the milliner's, Terrence the Topper now had six banana skins stuck up his brim. What? Oh, I'm so sorry, completely wrong story! That's *Hats on the Run*. Let me see. *Bats on the Run*, no, *Gnats on the Run*, no, *Pat's got the Runs*—no, no, no. Here we go! *Cats on the Run*, got it! Right.

Where were we? Oh yes, meanwhile, chez Burringo, Major was walking around, inspecting the apartment. The rather fresh breeze on the broomstick ride from the farm had not only blow-dried his hair in a very eighties fashion, it had also woken him from the concussed and confused coma into which the backwards-blasting bazooka had bolted him. Upon awakening of course, he had still been held by the scruff of his neck by Rodney, so there was nothing he could do but sit there and watch the world whizz by below him. Major found this experience strangely relaxing, and by the time he and Rodney arrived back in the apartment, he was more chilled than either of the witches. The dude was back in town.

'That's not Ginger!' screeched Janice when Rodney walked in with Major under his arm.

'No chips, Sherlock,' said Rodney. 'I know it's not Ginger. But it is a ginger cat and it's pretty smart. Look what it did to my hat!'

Janice gasped at the huge hole in her husband's helmet. 'He did that?' she asked. 'How?'

'I'll tell you tomorrow,' said Rodney. 'Come on, let's go to bed. I'm exhausted and it's getting light outside.'

True to her personality, Janice's laziness outweighed her curiosity. She let Rodney pick her up off the sofa and carry her up the stairs in a fireman's lift, which always made her giggle in a most revolting manner. This left Major downstairs alone, where he walked around, inspecting things. He tried out the sofa and found it suitably soft. He jumped up on the work surfaces and liked their lickability. He scratched at the stair carpet (scratchy enough), pushed his nose against the corner of the fridge (frigid enough), and played tennis with the blind cord (cordial enough).

'Mmm,' he thought. 'Mm-hm.'

You see, Major did like life at the stables, but he'd been there a long time, and ever since Ginger had left him, the place had never really felt like home. If these witches wanted to put him up for a bit, let him sleep on their sofa, and feed him twice a day, well, who was he to complain? And if he didn't like it, no doubt he could move on when he felt like it. And so, comforted by these life-threateningly mistaken thoughts, Major curled up on the sofa, which was still warm from Janice's saggy bottom. There he fell into a deep doze and dreamt all day dreams he had long forgotten. Who knows what it was about that place, but for some reason he dreamt only of the cat who had broken his heart and left his life listless and limp. When he awoke that evening, once again, for the first time in nearly a week, the flat was filled with the sound of big ginger sighs.

And where was the object of his dreams just then? Where indeed? Where wasn't she? And why wasn't she where she wasn't, and who wasn't she being when she wasn't there? Agh! See how annoying it is when people ask too many questions! Dear reader, if you ever find yourself asking too many questions, it's best just to stop, reflect (a mirror might help), and ask if you really need an answer. Which, of course, is another question, so be careful. **Bennyway**, let's get back to Ginger. It's getting dark, and she's all alone with nothing but her six empty bellies for company, and something creepy is about to happen.

It was getting dark and Ginger was tired again. She had been walking all day, following a winding country road that led towards the Great Dark Forest. Now, you're probably wondering why she was following the road, especially if it was winding. Wouldn't it have been quicker to cut across the fields in a straight line as the crow flies? Well, **humdy haw**, let's think about that one.

Firstly, grass tickles the tummy, and when you've got six bellies that's a lot of tickle. Secondly, rivers. Heard of them? What if Ginger hit a river, huh? Cats and water don't mix. And I don't mean in an oil-and-water, it's-OK-they-separate-again kind of way. Oh no. I mean they don't even talk to each other at parties. And thirdly, Ginger was trying to hitch-hike. Crazy, I know. Hitchhiking like that can get a cat as flat as a mat, but Ginger was in a hurry. She hadn't liked the look of that fire she'd seen the night before. Something was clearly wrong, and she needed to get back to Major ASAP.

So Ginger dragged her weary tiger-striped frame along that windy road all day, the sun climbing high in the sky and parching her throat. It was a very quiet road, and only two or three cars passed by. Each time she climbed up the grassy verge and stuck out a claw, but each time they sped past, empty but for the driver and with plenty of room for a cat, even one with six bellies. Selfish clods.

By late afternoon Ginger was a very tired pussy indeed. Oh, how her paws ached from the hot and gritty tarmac. Oh, how her bellies ached, inside from emptiness and outside from the scratchy thistles on the verge. She was beginning to regret not bringing Tuck along with her. Admittedly, he would have annoyed her all day with talk about the moon and mushroom blooming sauce. But right now she could have started looking forward to a light chocolate mouse or a vole roll. Three of her bellies rumbled at the very thought of this, but the other three were too tired to do even that. 'One more hill,' thought Ginger, for the road not only wound and weaved, it rose and fell too. 'One more hill and I'll stop.' So she dragged herself along the tarmac, on and on, until at the very top she found a gap in the hedge that ran alongside it.

What a view. Far back the way she had come she could see rolling green hills, the road a snaking, grey line that appeared here and there across it. In the very furthest distance she could make out some dark shapes, which must have been the city, and as she watched they started to glow as lights came on. To her left, west, the sky was burning and bruised as the sun's rays angled at the pollution and particles and petite, purply things that make a sunset. And ahead of her, stretching as far as the eye could see, lay the Great Dark Forest.

Gulp. There was no point in pushing on any more that day. She was more tired than a, than a . . . More tired than a tick in a . . . Oh lord, she was so tired she couldn't think what she was more tired than. She sat there struggling with it, watching the sun set to the west and the sky grow surprisingly dark to the east. She realised it was dark not only because the night was coming but because low black clouds were rolling in towards her. **Ooh nooooo**—a storm!

Ginger looked along the road, but the first trees of the forest were still quite a distance away. She'd never make it to them in time, even if she wasn't so tired. She hadn't passed any shelter on the way up the road either, and the hedgerow wasn't nearly thick enough to provide protection. Raindrops would drip deeply and drop damply down it and drench her. Drat! She looked towards the sunset, into the stubbly field that ran away from the road, but it was empty. What to do? Where else could she go? What do you think, dear reader? What should she do?

Turn around, Ginger darling. Look east! No, sweetheart, the other way. There we go. Ginger turned and looked at the grassy field beneath the ominous sky, its further reaches no longer green but already in dark shadow as the night and the storm rolled in. Halfway across it, no more than twenty metres away, sat an old pigsty. Without a second thought Ginger ran to it. Now, when cats walk through grass they step gingerly, as we know. Even if they're not ginger or Ginger, but if they are ginger and Ginger, they step very gingerly indeed. But when they run through grass it's a different story. They're low to the ground, flat, and fast. Or fat and fast in Ginger's case, but there's no need to get personal. Anyway, Ginger ran all the way to the pigsty. This was further than she'd run in quite a while, and when she arrived she was out of breath. She sat there with her mouth open and watched as the first fat drops of rain fell from the sky.

Suddenly there was a huge crack of thunder, *KERBOOM!* and the pigsty shook around her. Then it stopped shaking, but something beside her carried on moving. Something big. Ginger turned her head slowly but saw nothing but a few wooden planks nailed to the posts that held up the pigsty's roof. Straw was poking out from between the planks, and as she watched, the something big moved again on the other side of the wood. Ginger looked out at the rain, halfway to torrential already. She summoned up her courage, coughed slightly, and said, 'Hello?' There was no response, but the something big moved again, and she heard what sounded like a sneeze. 'Oh,' she thought. 'This is ridiculous', and she jumped up on top of the little wooden wall to see what was on the other side.

'Goodness!' she said out loud when she got up there. 'Pigs!'

She wasn't wrong. There stood two huge pigs, snuffling around in the straw and quite positively not looking at her.

'"Pigs,"' said one pig to the other. '"Pigs", she says. Like she was expecting to find a crocodile in a pigsty.'

'I'm sorry,' said Ginger. 'I thought this place was abandoned.'

'Really!' said the pig who had spoken first, the one closer to her. 'How very dare you! We had it decorated only last year.'

'Don't lower yourself, Beryl,' said the other pig. 'She looks like a stray and probably just wants some money.'

'Good luck with those bellies!' said the pig called Beryl. 'She'd struggle to raise a few pennies at a pension fund.'

I don't know about you, but I have no idea whatsoever what that means and nor did Ginger, but the two pigs found it very funny and chortled away at Ginger's expense.

Now, of course if you or I found two snobby pigs laughing at our bellies or our fundraising abilities, we'd be most upset. It's a strange rule of human life that you may not like someone, but you still want them to like you. But cats aren't like that, you see. Not if they're high up. If they're down on the ground or lying on the bed or even on the back of the sofa, oh yes—they want to be fussed! They want to be stroked and admired and told how cute and lovely they are. But any higher than waist height and they couldn't give a flying fox what you think of them. Pah, they can hardly even hear it.

So Ginger sat up on the wooden fence that ran around the pigsty and licked her chest while the rain hammered down on the corrugated iron overhead. Have you heard the noise rain makes on corrugated iron? It's loud! So loud that if you'd been there when I was telling you this story you wouldn't have even heard it. What? What did she find in the pigsty? A what? Who's Beryl? That kind of thing.

Fortunately, Ginger didn't mind the noise. She was just glad to be out of the horrible rain. She sat there, washing herself slowly, glancing occasionally at the two fat pigs and wondering what they were laughing about. Outside the sty, the grassy field turned slowly to mud, and soon the huge raindrops threw up big brown splashes when they landed. Then it grew even darker, and even with her cat's eyes Ginger struggled to see until suddenly the whole landscape was lit up in a flash of silver lightning. One thousand, two thousand, three thousand, *KERBOOOOOOM*, the thunder rolled in, and once more the pigsty shook so hard that Ginger nearly fell off the wooden fence. 'Mmm,' she thought. Maybe it wasn't such a good idea to sleep up there after all. So she jumped down to the straw on the non-pig side of the planks and was just getting settled again when she saw a movement in the corner of her eye.

A rat! Ginger didn't even think, she just did a quick sideways movement towards it. But before she was even halfway to it, the rat made a horrible squealing noise.

There was another great flash of lightning, and Ginger saw, to her disbelief and confusion, the rat dead on the floor in front of her, its neck open and shining red until the lightning ended and all was black again. Oo-er missus. Ginger didn't like the look of that. She was hungry alright, but whatever had killed that rat was dangerous, and what's worse, it was a lot faster than she was. She backed up towards the fence and sat wondering what to do. When the lightning flashed again, the rat was gone.

The rain was falling on the city too that night, but in the Burringos' apartment you could hardly hear it. Occasionally the wind would change direction and smatter it against the windows, but otherwise all was quiet. Rodney and Janice had gone out for an Indian meal (the Singh children from two streets down) and left Major all alone. They'd fed him before they'd left and even given him a saucer of milk, and now he sat on the warm, dry windowsill, thinking life was good.

Half an hour later he was still sitting there and thinking life was kind of nice. And another half an hour after that, he was sitting there as bored as bat's bits. Where were the mice darting across his stable floor? Where was the wind bending the trees overhead and scattering the courtyard with brittle debris? Where were the bats that used to dart in through the farmhouse window and tell him all the gossip from the countryside? He'd thought he needed a change and maybe he did, but not to this sterile apartment where nothing ever happened, with owners who slept all day and then went out at night. It was rubbish.

'Right,' Major thought. 'I'm outta here. Like a cat outta hell.' And he went and sat next to the apartment door, waiting for the Burringos to arrive home so he could say, 'See ya, wouldn't want to be ya', and head off home.

Well, I don't know about you, dear reader, but I see a slight conflict of values approaching, don't you? Don't you? Oh, you were kidding. Tch, you! Uh-oh, here it comes. It was two o'clock in the morning when Rodney and Janice stumbled home. They'd had a little too much to eat—having found themselves unsatisfied by the Singh children, they'd eaten the kids' Poppa(dom) and Ma(sala) too—and they'd had much too much to drink. Janice had a particular fondness for cherry brandy, which wasn't a fondness that the liqueur returned. It made her loud and not a little obnoxious when, as we know, she was normally so sweet and charming.

'Ooooh,' she said when she eventually managed to open the door to the apartment. 'Look who's 'ere to say 'ello. 'Ello, gingey puddy wuddy cat.'

Janice breathed cherry fumes all over Major, who was already a little grumpy at having to wait so long for her and Rodney to come home. He gave her his most withering stare, flicked his tail slightly, and walked between her legs and out of the apartment.

''Ere, where's 'e going?' said Janice, who always dropped her h's when she was drunk.

'Who?' said Rodney, h's fully intact. He hadn't seen that Major had sauntered between his legs too as he stumbled behind Janice into the apartment.

''Im! That fat ginger substitute—grab 'im!' screamed Janice.

Major thought that was rich. He was certainly broad-shouldered, but he'd never been fat in his life. 'Now listen here, wart-face,' he said. But that was all he got to say before Rodney turned, picked him up, and threw him back into the apartment.

'Do you mind!' said Major, in a serious grump now, and running back to the door. This time Janice grabbed him and gave him a smack on his haunch with the palm of her hand. Ouch! Can you imagine how painful it is for a cat to be hit by something as big as a witch? That would be like a huge giant slapping you across the ribs with a hand as big as a car. Ouch, ow, ow. Well, as you can imagine, Major wasn't going to take that without protest.

'**Eeeeeeeowwwwwwooooh**!' screamed Janice. ''E bit me! The miserable little doormat bit me!'

And she threw Major across the room. He landed on the kitchen table and was still steadying himself from the shock when he saw Rodney coming towards him, a distinctive tinge of green rising in his cheeks. Rodney had grabbed a broomstick which had been leaning against the living room wall, and now as he approached he raised it high above his head, narrowly missing the lampshade and even more narrowly missing Major as he slammed the twiggy end down on the table. *KERBANK!*

Major only just got out of the way in time—otherwise he would have been flat cat. He jumped down to the floor and crawled under the sofa, but within a second Rodney and Janice were on their knees, poking him out. Rodney was using the handle of the broomstick, and Janice was using a tennis racquet, which she had just magicked into existence.

'Get lost!' growled Major. 'Leave me alone!' Well, eventually they did, but only because it was all too much effort for Janice, and she was worried her cherry brandy and huge Indian meal might come up again.

'**Fuhgeddaboudit**,' she said to Rodney. 'Stupid blooming moggie. Let's go to bed.'

'Already?' said Rodney. 'It's not even light yet. Go on, let's skin him.'

'Nah,' said Janet. 'I'm cream-crackered. And besides, we need to keep 'im alive till we get the other one for the experiment. Oops.'

She put her hand over her mouth. Not because she'd done a big cherry brandy and Indian children burp but because Rodney had shot her a withering look. They weren't supposed to talk about the experiment in front of the cat.

'Yes,' said Rodney deliberately. 'Let's go to bed.'

An hour later the house was quiet again but for the sonorous sounds of sorcerers' snoring. Major dragged himself out from under the sofa and licked himself back into shape. 'Rattlesnakes,' he thought to himself. 'This place is seriously uncool. I have got to get me out of here.' He went and sniffed at the front door again, then had a good old scratch at the carpet to check the tunnelling options, which proved themselves clearly not-gonna-happen. He checked all the windows and even tapped the walls for weak points. Na-huh. He climbed the stairs and crept past the reverberating secret-upstairs-locked room door. No luck there either. The spare bedroom had a huge dent in the wall from an argument where Janice had thrown a Wedgwood statuette at Rodney, but it was no help. The flat was hermetically sealed.

'Oh dear,' said Major. For the first time it dawned on him that he was in serious trouble.

A BIT OF A SURPRISE

Well, where would you rather be right now? Locked in a hermetically sealed apartment with two witches whose only reason for not skinning you is that they want to put your brain into another body? Or stuck in a pigsty in the middle of a rainstorm with a mysterious rat-murdering monster? Now, this may be an everyday dilemma for you. Maybe this is one of those decisions where you'd have to think for, hmm, thirty seconds and then make up your mind. If so, bully for you. Me, I ain't so sure. Ginger, I can tell you, would have gone for the apartment option just then. Things had got a little hairier since we last saw her, you see. The pigs were not helping. She'd tried jumping in with them, thinking whatever huge carnivorous beast was out in the dark would surely go for bacon over cat gut, if only from the point of view of quantity over quality.

'Get your furry frame out of my straw!' said the pig whose name she didn't know as soon as she saw her.

'You tell her, Mildred,' said the other one, which at least sorted out the name problem.

'I mean it,' said Mildred. 'You scram now or I'm going to bite you.' And she bared her horrible piggy-yellow teeth. Now, if you know anything about pigs, you probably know this, but just in case you don't I'm going to tell you. Pigs bite! And when they bite they don't stop until they can feel their teeth crunching against each other.

'But there's a big carnivorous monster out there,' said Ginger. 'You can't send me back out there.'

'You mind your cheek, young lady,' said Mildred, taking a step forwards. 'I mean it, I'll bite.'

Well, seeing as you're so good with these decisions, why don't you decide? Stay in the pen with the teeth-baring pigs or expose yourself to a huge carnivorous rat-killing monster? Huh? Well, unfortunately, you weren't there for Ginger to consult, otherwise I'm sure she'd have taken notes and considered your feedback. Instead she spat somewhat disrespectfully at Mildred in that way that cats do sometimes and jumped back up onto the wooden fence that ran around the pen. Behind her she heard Mildred say, 'You see, Beryl, you have to take a firm trotter with these cats. It's the only language they understand.'

'Mmm,' said Beryl. '**Scroffle scroffle oink oink**.'

Ginger ignored them. Instead she stared down at the straw on the other side of the enclosure, sodden with muddy raindrops. There lay another four rats, all dead and looking somewhat surprised. And out in the dark of the wild wet night, she saw two huge green eyes. And then, as she watched in terror, she saw some brilliant white teeth appear below them. The teeth moved slowly apart, and a pinky-pink tongue flicked between them as the teeth's owner said, 'Surprise!' And with that a very muddy, very wet, and very happy-looking Tuck jumped in out of the rain.

'Hiya!' he said. 'Did I surprise you? Did I? Look at all the mice I got. How are you? What's in there? Is it pigs?'

Well, I struggle to describe all the emotions that ran through Ginger at that moment. She was firstly furious at her feline friend for frightening the flipping fur off her. Secondly, she was surprisingly serene at the serendipitous sensation of seeing him again. Thirdly, she was hungry. Mighty, mighty hungry.

'Oh,' she said. 'I was wondering when you'd turn up. Do you want me to sashimi these for you while you freshen up?'

'Ooh, yes please,' said Tuck. 'I might just have a little shower before dinner. You should do it too. You know how dirty pigs are.'

'Well, really!' Ginger heard Beryl say. 'How rude!'

'Disgusting,' said Mildred in return. 'I really cannot wallow in these conditions.'

But Tuck didn't hear them. He was outside again, singing in the rain.

'Pigs are dirty,
Girls are flirty,
I once had a little friend called Bertie.
Bertie ate a spoon,
He died too soon,
They put him in a rocket ship and sent him to the moon.'

'That doesn't even make sense,' thought Ginger as she sliced up the rats, but she didn't mind. She was too relieved that she was about to eat and not be eaten, and truth be told, not a little curious about how Tuck had turned up in the night.

'Well,' said Tuck as he licked the last of the rat's tail off his lips. 'It was all feline fine at first. I felt funny in my tummy when you said goodbye, but then the barn cats woke up and we played I spy, which is this really complicated and difficult game. Then we slept again, which was exhausting. Then, when we woke up, we got talking about ambitions, and I said I wanted to find the mushroom sauce, and they said what do you mean, and I said how we'd come to the moon to look for mushroom sauce and—' Tuck paused and to Ginger's huge surprise she saw he was crying. 'And . . . and . . . and . . .' He was sobbing so hard he could hardly talk.

'Do keep it down, you foul moggies!' said Mildred.

'Oh shush, Mildred,' said Beryl. 'Can't you see the little thing's upset?'

I can't tell you the look that Mildred gave Beryl at this point because they're inside the wooden pen and the action's happening on the outside, but I'm guessing it wasn't pretty.

'Oh dear,' said Ginger. 'What did they say?'

'Waaah!' said Tuck. 'They said we weren't on the moon and that even if we were, it wouldn't matter because the moon wasn't—*sniff*—**waahhh** . . . they said it wasn't even made of mushroom sau-or-oor-oooorce.'

'What did he say about the moon?' said Mildred.

'See?' said Beryl. 'You're interested too now.'

'Everything's a competition with you, isn't it, Beryl,' said Mildred, and the two pigs got into a real oink-off so that for a while they didn't hear a word the cats were saying.

'It's not true, is it?' said Tuck, wiping his nose on his paw and looking over it at Ginger. 'We are on the moon, aren't we?'

'Well . . . ,' said Ginger. 'Strictly speaking . . .'

'Waaaah,' said Tuck. 'Waaah. . . . Even if we weren't on the moon I'd want you to pretend we were just so I don't feel this bad. And even if it wasn't made of mushroom sauce I'd want to believe it was so I could look forward to having lots and lots of it until I couldn't eat any more.'

'Are you sure?' said Ginger.

Tuck nodded slowly. He was gulping and snotty and too upset to say anything else.

'Well then,' said Ginger. 'That's easy. Yes, we are on the moon. And yes, it is made of mushroom sauce. We just need to find a lake or some other surface where the moon's crust is shallow enough for sauce to still be sitting.'

'Really?' said Tuck, his eyes flashing green with pleasure. 'Is it really true? Really?'

'Er . . .' said Ginger. 'Ooh, look, there's another piece of rat's tail which you haven't eaten yet.'

Then, before Tuck had time to finish swallowing the tail end of the meal, she asked him how he'd found her.

'Well,' he said. 'I knew you were following the road. So I ran and ran and ran until I could see you. That took about ten minutes, so I thought I'd follow you and make you jump. Then it started raining and you came in here, and then I saw the mice and I thought you'd be hungry. Ha ha. I scared you, didn't I?'

'What?' said Ginger. 'Scared? Me? What on earth gave you that idea?'

'You told that fat pig in there that a huge, big monster was out there.'

'How rude!' said Mildred, who'd started listening again. 'Beryl, that cat called you fat, did you hear?'

'But there is a big monster out there,' said Ginger.

'What?' said Tuck, his eyes huge and yellow again. 'Oh no! Oh no, really! Oh how absolutely **teddifying.** How awful. Die! We're all going to die!'

'Is this to do with the moon again?' said Beryl.

Ginger managed to calm Tuck down. She told him she'd look after him all night. All he had to do was lie still and let her use him as a pillow, and they'd both be fine.

'Oh, thank you ever so much,' said Tuck as he curled up tight to his tail. 'For the moon and the protection and everything.'

'It's nothing,' said Ginger. 'Nothing at all. Except, Tuck, about the sauce . . .'

But Tuck was already snoring, deep in dreams which, given his tenuous grasp on reality at the best of time, are ideally left undescribed.

🐾 YET ANOTHER BIT

The next morning dawned bright and early. Well, not that early. Just before sunrise really, which if you think about it, is neither early nor late but pretty much bang on time. Lord, imagine if dawn had an opportunity to be early or late. You'd be up and ready for school, and it might not even be midnight yet.

Bennyway! The next morning dawned bright and bang on time. Cocks crowed, other birds chirped, and the two pigs snuffled and scuffled and scratched themselves. The cats rose early, and before the sun had properly squeezed itself up into the sky, they were back on the road. At a little before ten o'clock they reached the Great Dark Forest. Here the road veered to the right as if the trees were too ominous to drive through, but a faint path continued straight into the dark green shadows. A huge sign stood over the path. It said: 'Great Dark Forest'. And underneath it was written: 'Scary Path'.

'Ooh,' said Tuck. 'Isn't there another way?'

'No,' said Ginger. She said it so quickly and curtly that if you didn't know her better, you might think she was a bit scared herself and was just summoning up her courage before it ran back down the road, past the barn, into the city and jumped into the tiger-striped taxi and drove them both back to the apartment.

'Come on,' she said. 'We'll be fine.'

And so they strode on, the tarmac below their paws replaced by rough ground still soft from the night's storm. Then, as they entered the forest proper, the soft ground was replaced by dry, dusty soil that the rain hadn't even reached, so thick was the canopy overhead. Even the daylight struggled through the thick treetops, and soon the air around them was as dull as a winter's evening. On either side of the path wild vines and rough ferns covered the forest floor, and here and there ominous holes appeared, homes to strange animals the cats could only guess at. They found huge spiders' webs and dusty snake tracks, the fallen corpses of once majestic trees, and the skeletons of long-dead birds. When a breeze blew, the whole forest moved with it, one part after the other, the way the ocean responds to a wave.

But mostly the forest was silent, dark, and waiting, and the two cats had the constant impression that they were being watched. Still they padded on. The path died out after a while, but the cats had no need of it. Cats have a sense of direction which is beyond the understanding of humans, so that even if I explained it to you, you still wouldn't get it. As senses go, it's not perfect but it is very good. Ginger knew where she wanted to get to, and so she followed her instinct. And Tuck knew he didn't want to be alone in the G.D.F. so he followed Ginger.

At noon they had a little rest, the sun directly overhead but barely detectable through the thick green roof of the trees. They found a puddle and lapped at it, but the water was stagnant and something about that place unnerved them, and so they walked on. On and on, past endless watchful trees, timeless and placeless and nameless, only the cats' instinct telling them they were moving in a line and not a circle. All too soon the light inside the forest began to fade, and the cats realised it was evening. It was that time of year when nights draw in more quickly than you expect (daylight savings had just ended), and before Ginger and Tuck were really aware of it, they found they were walking in the dark. It was then that they discovered the forest wasn't empty at all.

Back at the apartment Major was feeling grumpy. He'd tried weeing in all the corners of the living room to see if that made him feel any better, but it didn't. He sprayed all over the dishes drying in the rack, and that didn't help either. He scratched the carpet by the front door again, chewed the corners of a few coffee-table books and even did a poo on the kitchen benchtop, but none of it improved his mood. There was nothing for it—he was going to have to find something precious and break it.

But could he find something precious and breakable? Could he buffalo! There were no knick-knacks, vases, or lamps in sight. He was ten years too late, you see. Had Janice kidnapped him before she met Rodney, for example, Major would have had a dense display of delicates at his disposal. As a single woman, Janice had been more than partial to small figurines, and her collection had included chinaware from all over the world. But in the early years of the Burringos' marriage she had thrown them all at Rodney. Few had hit their target but all had smashed. Now there was little left for Major to break. Or so he thought, until on the desk near the window he spotted the computer. 'Aha!' he thought. 'That's definitely breakable.' He decided to spring up onto the desk so he could squeeze himself between the computer and the wall. A good heave-ho, shove-oh, give it all you've got-oh ought to do it.

But as Major jumped up, he accidentally trod on the keyboard and the monitor flickered to life. And what did he see there? He saw Janice Burringo's screensaver photograph. It was a particularly irksome family photograph which the Burringos had used for their Christmas cards the year before, not realising this was an incredibly cheesy thing to do. Oh yes it is. The photograph showed Janice and Rodney dressed up in Santa outfits, and on their laps, also dressed as Santas, were their two cats. Tuck on Rodney's lap, Ginger on Janice's. Major shook his head and looked again. That looked like his Ginger in a Santa outfit. He put his nose close to the screen, then jumped down and ran to the other side of the room to get some perspective. That *was* his Ginger. '**Owemjee**!' he thought. '**Owembuffalojee**!'

It took Major only twenty-two goes to guess Janice's password. After trying all the names he'd heard her call Rodney, he tried the two local football teams, her date of birth, and what he already knew to be her favourite food (chocolate-dipped baby). Then he tapped 'warts', all lower-case one word, and ta-da, the screensaver was replaced by the last thing Janice had looked at: a rather racy picture of her favourite boyband, Mirrorsplatter.

Major used his nose and his paws to type as quickly as he could. This still wasn't very quick—it would be like you or me typing with grapes—but it was quick enough. He went into Janice's Spookle search history to see what he could find. And what did he find? He found searches for commingling of cats, pictures of Purraris, and the location spell. You see, Rodney and Janice shared a profile, so it was all in there, no holds barred, nothing hidden.

Still, for Major it raised more questions than it answered. What was he doing there if they had Ginger? Where was Ginger? What were they wanting to commingle? What Major thought was this: 'Mm-hm.' And then, 'Mm-hm-hmm.' He jumped down and sniffed the whole flat through again. Now he knew why he had dreamt of Ginger all day when he'd thought he'd got over her years ago. The whole place carried her scent.

Well, poor old Major. Can you imagine the emotions of sadness and loss this stirred in him? All the years he'd been missing Ginger and wondering what he could have done differently, and she'd been here all that time. Against her will? He couldn't imagine her liking this place. But . . . well . . . maybe . . . oh . . . He pushed his feelings to one side. The point was, Ginger had been here, and so had another cat. It must be the stupid-looking one in the screensaver picture. But they'd escaped. What had Janice said about an experiment?

So on and so forth Major went, asking himself lots of questions which you know the answers to so I won't bore you with them. He thought and thought and thought and searched and Spookled and did some sums, and suffice to say by the time it grew dark outside the apartment windows, he'd worked it all out: the experiment, the attempt to make a Purrari, all of it. All except one thing: How had Ginger escaped? And how had she ended up in the flat in the first place? OK, that's two things. But everything else Major had worked out. And boy, did it make him grumpy.

'What was that noise?' said Tuck. He sat up and looked around him. There was very little light on the forest floor, for only the thinnest of moon rays could make their way through the treetops. In their frail silvery light the forest looked like a crackly old black-and-white movie.

'It was nothing,' said Ginger through her tail, which she'd wrapped over her face to keep warm.

'That's what you said last time.'

'And what was it last time?'

'Can't remember.'

'Tuck, it was nothing. Go back to sleep.'

Tuck lay down again and snuggled closer to Ginger. As night had fallen, the air in the forest had grown colder, and despite their recent outdoor adventures, neither cat had a full winter coat yet. Ginger closed her eyes and seemed to sleep again, but poor Tuck thought he'd never been so cold or so frightened. Five minutes later he miaowed again.

'What was that noise?' he said.

Ginger opened her eyes so she could roll them and ignore him. But then she heard a noise too. It was a slow shuffling, which a minute before she'd thought was a breeze in the trees. But now it was closer, and when she put her ear to the ground (not something you see cats doing very often), she could hear it was footsteps. Footsteps coming their way. She stood up and looked in the direction of the noise.

'Look!' said Tuck. 'Look! There's something over there!'

Ginger looked, her eyes less sharp than Tuck's, and soon she made out a skinny figure with a big fat tail.

'Oh no,' she said.

'What is it?' said Tuck.

But by now the animal, whose ribs were showing through his fur and was looking very hungry, was close enough to answer for himself.

'I'm a fox,' he said, in a velvety English accent. 'Crosby Snarlsgood, to be precise. How the devil do you do?'

'Hiya!' said Tuck. 'We're very well, thank you. Phew. We thought you were something scary.'

Ginger elbowed Tuck in his ribs, but Tuck just carried on talking.

'We're going to see Ginger's old boyfriend and get some mushroom sauce on the way. Are you a flying fox?'

'Only when I'm happy,' said the fox. 'Are you lost?'

'No,' said Ginger, her voice level and low. 'We're fine, thank you.'

'Are you sure? I'd be more than happy to help you.

Maybe you'd like to come back to my lair. I'm sure my family would be delighted to have you over for dinner.'

'Ooh, yes please!' said Tuck. 'What's on the menu?'

'Mushroom sauce,' said the fox, who, being a fox, was quick on the uptake and singularly sly. 'We have so much of it in our house we barely know what to do with it. Ladles and ladles of it.'

Well, you can guess what colour Tuck's eyes went when he heard this. Greener than a seasick and jealous emerald in a lush field of grass.

'This way,' said the fox. 'As I said, Snarlsgood's the name. And you are?'

'Am I?' said Tuck, walking after him and then wondering why he couldn't walk any further.

'I mean what's your name?'

But Tuck was too preoccupied to answer. He wanted to know why he couldn't move forward. He turned and saw Ginger had sat her full weight on his tail. The fox seemed to have forgotten he'd asked Tuck his name and carried on walking forwards, talking softly to the big black cat, who he thought was right behind him.

'Tuck,' said Ginger sternly but almost in a whisper. 'Do you know what a fox's favourite food is?'

'**Owee**, get off my tail, Ginger. It hurts.'

'Answer the question and then I'll get off. What do foxes like to eat?'

'Mushroom sauce.'

'Wrong,' said Ginger. 'If foxes love mushroom sauce so much, why are they giving it away? Tuck, what is a fox's favourite food?'

'Oh, hang on,' said Tuck. 'I know this one. How does it go? Ooh, ooh, I haven't heard it in ages. Oh, I remember:

'Spiders eat lice,
Cats eat mice,
Birds eat spiders
Without thinking twice.
Dogs eat bones
And live in big boxes.
Witches eat children
And men hunt foxes.
Foxes eat cats,
Cats eat rats,
Rats spread disease,
And that's about that.'

'Ha! I remembered it, Ginger. Bet you thought I wouldn't. A fox's favourite food is—oh! Oh, oh! Oh let me go, Ginger! We have to—'

'What is it?' said the fox, who had turned at the noise Tuck was making and suddenly realised Tuck was no longer behind him. He stood about three metres away from the cats, his narrow eyes sparkling in the thin moonlight. 'What the devil are you two doing back there?'

'Just one second, Mr Snotgood,' Ginger called out to him. Then in a very hushed tone she said to Tuck: 'Listen to me. You have to do precisely what I say, do you understand?'

But Tuck didn't seem to understand anything. He was snivelling and whimpering and trying with all his might to pull his tail from under the weight of Ginger and her six bellies.

'Tuck.'

'It's a fox!' he hissed at her. 'A nasty, evil fox.'

Ginger sighed heavily and tried to ignore the fox, who was clearly getting impatient. 'Do hurry up, people,' he was saying. 'Mrs Snarlsgood does so hate to eat late.'

Ginger leant slightly, not wanting to take her weight off Tuck's tail, and gave Tuck a full sideswipe across his whiskers. Biff. Just like that. Now he was listening.

'You must do exactly as I say,' she repeated. 'Do you understand?'

Tuck nodded.

'Repeat it.'

'It,' said Tuck.

'No, I mean, oh don't worry. Listen, when I say go, you must run as fast as you can around that tree.'

She pointed at a tired, old gum tree fifty metres away. Tuck stared after her paw into the gloom and didn't see the suspicious fox edging nearer. 'And then,' Ginger said, 'around that one over there'. She pointed to the left to a huge fallen oak and watched over Tuck's shoulder as the fox got closer still. 'And finally,' she said, miaowing more quickly now, 'over-to-that-one-and-straight-back-here-as-fast-as-you-can. Faster than you've ever run. Are you ready?'

The fox was really close now, and Ginger could see him jostling his haunches ready to pounce. She lifted her weight off Tuck's tail and shouted, 'Go! Run, Tuck! He's right behind you!'

Do you remember earlier in the story that I said Tuck would run far faster than he did down the corridor outside the Burringos' apartment to the lift? You don't? Well, I did, and this is the bit where he does it. And so would you if you were a cat and you had a big posh fox on your tail! Tuck jumped over a log and around a root and past a puddle and under a twig and over a mound and all of it faster than you could say, 'Je suis perdu à Paris sans une parapluie'.

On and on Tuck ran, the first tree much further in the twilight than he'd thought, even though he was running faster than he'd ever run in his admittedly not-very-long life. The details of the forest blurred either side of him, parallel streaks of brown and darker brown and maybe green, but all of it in the pale half-light looking a bit dark-browny. Faster and faster and faster. But foxes have longer legs than cats, and hunger can make you run faster than you'd think, especially when you see your dinner running away from you. Put a burger on a pair of legs and see how you react. No sooner was Tuck over that first log than Crosby Snarlsgood was after him, teeth champing only centimetres from Tuck's tail.

By the time Tuck got to the first tree, the fox was little more than five centimetres behind him. Tuck could feel the fox's hot, hungry breath, the foul smell of flesh-tearing teeth, the evil, rabid violence of carnivorous intent. '**Noooo**!' he miaowed, and ran even faster because fear is the greatest accelerator of all, even greater than hunger. Tuck zoomed into warp speed, whizzing between tree trunks, bypassing bushes, racing over dead leaves that flew up behind him in a cloud of, well, leaves. Whoosh! He was around the fallen tree trunk Ginger had pointed out, but still Snarlsgood was close behind, having cheated slightly and not gone all the way around the full trunk.

And where was Ginger during all of this? You remember that very first log Tuck jumped over? Come on, it was only ten lines ago. Well, Ginger jumped over it too, but then she stayed on the other side. She was one clever pussy, and she knew that the fox wouldn't resist chasing his dinner down, focusing 100 per cent on Tuck and forgetting about her completely. How right she was.

She sat with her back to the log with a big stick in her paws and watched the hunt. Watched with wide eyes as Snarlsgood nearly caught Tuck by the tail and then, with wider eyes still as they turned into the final straight, and it's Tuck on the outside by a nose and Snarlsgood's coming up to meet him, and no, Tuck has got away again, and there's only twenty metres in it, and they're on the final few metres of the most amazing race of the year, folks! Closer and closer they came, far faster than Ginger had even expected, and Tuck jumped straight over her and over the log behind her, and then Snarlsgood jumped too, and she shoved the stick she'd been holding high into the air above her.

When a fox running at full hunting speed trips in a forest in the middle of the night, does it make a sound? Yes, it blooming well does. It goes *bang,* **crash, wallop, cacrumble,** *snap, crump, crump,* **caproomph - crash,** tinkle-tinkle **boomph!!! Bang.** *Clatter-clatter bump.*

Ginger peered over the log, hoping desperately it was only Snarlsgood that had made this racket and that he hadn't caught up Tuck in his cacophonous carnage. But it didn't look good. All she could see was a broad trail of leafless ground with broken twigs thrown up either side. At the end of this trail was a crumple of fur with little stars circling above it. There was no sign of Tuck. Ginger climbed up slowly onto the log and peered back towards the dark and silent trees. Hopefully, the fur she could see was brown and foxy and not black and Tucky. She peered closer still.

'Tuck?' she called. 'Tuck, are you OK?'

'**Hiyaaaa**!' said Tuck, jumping up from the other side of the log. 'Surprise!'

'Cheeses!' said Ginger as every single hair on her body stood on end. 'Don't do that. I thought . . . Well, I thought I was very clever just then.'

'Me too,' said Tuck. 'I jumped down behind the log, and he must have tripped, and I've killed him.'

Ginger did one of those big ginger sighs I keep talking about and rolled her eyes. 'He might not be dead,' she said. 'Go and check.'

'No,' said Tuck.

'Go on.'

'No.'

'Who tripped the fox?'

'Ginger did.'

'That's right,' said Ginger, and she hopped down onto Tuck's side of the log and started walking gingerly up the trail which the tumbling Snarlsgood had left in his wake. She managed about four steps, which is only one step really if you count all four paws.

'No,' she said. 'Not dead. Just unconscious. You can tell by the stars. If he was dead, there'd be a little foxy angel with a harp floating upwards. We'd better get out of here.'

Tuck did not disagree, and so the two cats hopped back over the log and walked on deeper into the forest. Not the way their noses told them they should go, because the fox might come after them that way, him having instincts too. Instead they went off to the right a bit and then winding in and out of huge trees and under thick bracken and finally crawling under thick and thorny brambles. By the time they were too tired to walk any further they were completely and utterly lost.

BLOOMING HECK, IT'S ANOTHER BIT

MIAOWNWHILE, back at Burringo Towers, the witches had woken up.

'Pooh,' said Janice. 'There's a poo!'

'Oui,' said Rodney. 'There's a wee!'

'Scratch that!' they both yelled together. 'Look at our stair carpet!'

'That cat is pure evil,' said Rodney, searching for a paper towel under the sink with one hand and pointing at Major with the other. 'Evil and bad.'

'Evil and horrible and awful,' said Janice.

'In fact,' said Rodney, 'he's perfect!'

'Too darling for words,' said Janice, and before Major could react she'd swooped him up in her skinny arms. 'Oh, my preciously poisonous pussy,' she said. 'You're going to make the purrrfect Purrari.'

Major gave her his best attempt at a smile, but he couldn't bring himself to say anything and so bit her instead.

'Ooh!' said Janice, dropping him to the floor in that way that all cats hate. 'Ooh, he bit me! Terrible, terrible, awful, dreadful, marvellous, perfect cat!'

'Janice,' said Rodney, 'do calm down or you'll—'

But it was too late. The apartment was filling with Janice's green bum gas. 'I can't help it.' She laughed.

'I'm so excited. Darling Rodders, let's go and find ourselves a black cat straight away. We have everything we need for the mingle. Please? Pwease, Rodder Dodder, pwease can we?'

'You must be off your buffalo,' said Rodney, picking up the cat poo from the kitchen surface and throwing it into a bag for distribution at a later date. 'I'm cream-crackered. The last thing I want to do is go down to the dog home and get another blooming cat. You go if you're so keen, but leave me out of it.'

Ouch. Did I mention that Rodney wasn't an early-evening kind of person? Some people really are at their worst when they first wake up, and some witches are no different. Well, Janice was far too excited to let some miserable grotbag of a husband burst her bubble.

'Fine,' she said. 'I will! Just you watch.'

'I'm watching,' said Rodney.

And he was. He sat himself down on the sofa without washing his hands, crossed his arms, and watched Janice find her purse (English), put it in her purse (American), purse her lips, give him a rude gesture, and walk out the front door. Major watched all of this with great interest, and as Janice left he went running after her as fast as he could. But before he could make it out of the apartment, Janice had slammed the door behind her. Boy, did that make him grumpy.

It was a little over an hour later when Major heard Janice returning. Have you ever noticed how cats can do that? They can hear people coming before humans can. It's a quality they share with dogs (much to their disgust) and is not—as you may have assumed—based on their animal sixth sense. It's based in fact on the fact that factually their faculty of hearing is better than ours. They hear at much higher frequencies and can distinguish between the jingle jangle of keys at a distance greater than we could ever imagine. So there. But Major didn't hear only a jangle of keys approaching from outside the apartment door. There was another noise too, a squeaking, wiry noise that sounded suspiciously like a cage with a cat in it.

'I'm hungry,' said Tuck.

He and Ginger had awoken in a strange part of the forest. For the most part there were very few plants on the ground, just huge bare trunks of trees that stretched way up into the sky with, here and there, thick patches of rough grass, great tufts of grey-green blades which drooped or swooped as a breeze came through. It was noticeably cooler here than in the thicker parts of the G.D.F. and certainly the coldest temperature they'd experienced since leaving the apartment. It was as if summer had become exhausted overnight, given up the fight, and handed things over to autumn. On the few occasions when they could see through the canopy high above them, all they could see were dark, grey clouds.

'I'm hungry,' said Tuck again.

'And tired?' said Ginger.

'Yes!' said Tuck. 'How did you know?'

'Because you've told me about a hundred times since we first woke up. Shut up for goodness sake and keep walking.'

Now this sounded a little harsh even to Ginger, who was a harsh cat. So after a few minutes she said, 'Try not think about it'. She might well have said it to her own bellies too. 'I'm even hungrier than him', they said one after the other, although of course they said it in Tummeze, which sounds to you and me just like gurgling and rumbling. Tuck's stomach called back to them, as hungry tummies often do, and as the cats walked slowly through the forest, it sounded to the ants and lice like a storm approaching. On and on Ginger and Tuck walked, their sense of direction totally thrown but somehow still guiding them in vaguely the right direction. Or at least they hoped so.

It was a long, dry day. They left the half-grassy forest behind and entered a part of the wood with nothing but bare dirt on the ground. Then they left that for a part where the huge trees were replaced by medium-size trees. Then, towards the end of the day, they found they were walking downhill. To their joy they found a little creek. They hadn't realised how thirsty they were, and they lapped at the clear, cold water in long and lazy licks. Tuck would have purred, but he was too tired and hungry to do even that.

'It's nice, isn't it?'

'Yes,' said Tuck.

'What?' said Ginger.

'You said it was nice,' said Tuck.

'No, you said it was nice.'

'I didn't say that.'

'Well, if you didn't say it and I didn't say it . . .'

Both cats stopped drinking and looked up slowly to see who had said the water was nice. They hoped to goodness it wasn't a fox. They looked over the stream and saw nothing. They both looked to the left and saw nothing. Then they both looked to the right and saw nothing. Then they both looked behind them and saw . . . nothing! Just trees as far as they could see, medium-size trees nearby, bigger trees beyond them, a group of four knobbly saplings right behind them.

'Ooh dear, don't stop drinking on my account,' said the voice again.

Well, where else was there to look? No! Not down! Not unless you think worms and woodlice are wont to willingly woo you by wantonly wanging on and wasting words about water. No, no, no. Both cats looked *up*, and there, right above them, they saw a huge, furry animal with massive great antlers. Those four saplings behind the cats hadn't been saplings at all but legs—furry legs with hooves on one end and a massive great stag on the other.

'Agh!' yelled Tuck. 'It's a huge furry television transmitter monster!' and he jumped backwards over the creek in a not unimpressive double salto. Ginger rolled her eyes and—you guessed it—sighed.

'Ooh dear,' said the deer. 'What's wrong with him, dearie?'

'He's never seen a deer,' said Ginger to the deer. 'Not in your way, are we?'

'Ooh no, dearie,' said the deer. 'There's plenty for everyone, I'm sure. You two *are* a long way from home aren't you? You lost, need any help?'

Well, as you can see, the deer seemed pleasant enough, so Ginger told him their story while Tuck looked on warily from the other side of the stream. He couldn't stop staring at the deer's huge antlers, which were, it has to be said, quite extravagant.

'What are they for?' Tuck said at last, when Ginger had reached a pause in her story and was having another sip of water.

'What, dearie?' said the deer.

Tuck pointed up at the antlers, and the deer snorted.

'Well, dear,' he said. 'Don't tell anyone, but I use mine for getting national radio and drying my undies. Some boys use them to fight with, but I can't be doing any of that. They're furry—would you like to feel one, dear?'

It didn't seem quite proper to do so, but it didn't seem polite to refuse, so when the deer stepped into the stream and dipped his head towards Tuck, Tuck reached up a paw and stroked the antlers.

'Ooh,' he said, 'furry.'

'He he he,' said the deer. 'Careful dear, it tickles.' Then he said, 'Ooh, I have an idea', and before Tuck knew quite what was happening, the deer had taken another step forward and swooped him up in his antlers. 'Look, dear,' said the deer. 'You can probably see much further now and find your way home.'

Ginger put her paws in her ears and closed her eyes, waiting for Tuck to scream or panic and sink his claws in and for the deer to throw him off and make him scream even more. But unless she'd stuck her paws too far down her ears, none of this seemed to happen. She opened first one eye and then the other and pointed them both up at the deer's antlers. Tuck was sitting up there, beaming.

'Ginger!' he yelled down when he could see she was looking. 'This is brill! Look how high up I am. I can climb trees, look. It's so, it's so, it's so **cooooooooooool**!'

Well, of course Ginger did a big gingery sigh and rolled her eyes, but when the deer asked her if she'd like a go too, she said, 'Yeah, sure, why not. Nothing better to do. Might as well. Just to make Tuck feel more comfortable. S'pose.'

And within seconds there stood the deer with his huge and extravagant antlers each holding a hungry cat. 'Would you like to go somewhere?' he said.

'Don't suppose you know where there's any rats?' said Ginger.

'Rats? No, dear. Lots of good grass I can take you to, though.'

'Birds?' said Ginger.

'Ooh dear, you kitty-cats feeling peckish? I know just the place. Just over that hill in the distance there's a small lake where the birds bathe and drink. If we leave now, we should arrive just in time for breakfast. By the way, my name's Dozer. Shall we . . . ?'

As Dozer ambled through the trees and told Tuck and Ginger all about life in the forest, they both forgot their hunger completely. Neither of them had ever heard such stories, and although Ginger pretended she had, Tuck asked hundreds of questions about voles and weasels and ferns and burrows and pine cones and fireflies and bushfires, and oh, oh, oh, it sounded so exciting. It was only some hours later, when they had crossed over the hill and the sky had grown lighter and they could see the lake in the distance that either of them even thought about the birds they were going to have for breakfast.

'What is a bird?' said Tuck. 'Is it a kind of flower?'

'You're funny,' said Dozer.

'Nah, just stupid,' said Ginger.

'I am *not* stupid,' said Tuck. 'I am not. You take that back.'

'I tell you what,' said Ginger. 'You see how many of these funny animals you can catch when we get to the lake and I'll not only take it back, I promise to never ever say it again. But you'll have to catch at least four. And I warn you—you've got only once chance. One mistake and they'll not come back.'

'Are they rats?' said Tuck, giggling slightly as Dozer tripped on a little stone and made his antlers wobble.

'You'll see,' said Ginger. 'Now shush. I want to get some shut-eye before we arrive.' And with that she dropped into a deep doze, her paws tucked over her bellies and her chin deep in her chest. Dozer seemed to be sleeping too, as he walked, with his eyes closed and his breathing heavy. But Tuck was far too excited to sleep.

When they arrived at the lake, the two cats said goodbye to Dozer and thanked him for carrying them overnight. He asked if they were sure they wouldn't like to stay in the forest, but even Tuck knew this wasn't possible. They had to get back to Major's farm as fast as possible to see what had become of him. So Dozer said a final goodbye and walked away through the trees, Tuck waving hard until long after he was out of sight. Then the two cats hid, and Ginger told Tuck all about birds.

Now, I know you might think it's weird that Tuck doesn't know about birds, but remember, he grew up in a cage and then went straight from there to an apartment. Until he and Ginger escaped, he knew about sky only because he'd heard people talk about it. Expecting Tuck to know about birds is like expecting you to know about bivalves. Exactly.

So Ginger told him all about them (birds, not bivalves). About their wings and how they could fly, about how feathery and flitty and flighty and fiendishly difficult to catch they were. She was so hungry she could barely bring herself to talk about how meaty and chewy and tasty-yummy they were too. But she forced herself whilst Tuck listened with eyes even wider than the last time he was wide-eyed (which wasn't that long ago), and by the time the first few birds arrived at the stream, he was fully pumped for action. What could possibly go wrong?

A CHEEKY BIT

Parallels, parallels, will they never cease? From one hungry ginger cat desperately awaiting breakfast to another, this one slightly paler and locked in a witches' apartment back in the city. Zoom out, pan left very fast, zoom in again, and there we are. Poor Major had had a terrible night of it. Like his long-lost love he was hungry and tired and desperate for his num-nums. The night before, Janice and Rodney had had a horrible fight.

'What,' said Rodney, as soon as Janice walked through the door, 'is that?!'

He pointed with his fast-hooking nose at the cage she held in her hand.

'It's a cat,' she said.

'I know it's a cat, you stupid witch,' said Rodney. 'But you were supposed to get a sleek, black, athletic cat. That . . . that . . . that thing is none of the above.'

Well, Janice was exhausted from being on her feet all the way up in the elevator and in no mood for being yelled at by Rodney. So she screamed back at him about there not being any black ones available as they were all sick, and she liked this one, and what had he ever done for her anyway, and didn't she have a right to choose the cat she wanted, etcetera etcetera **etceterargh**.

While they were screaming and throwing insults at

each other (there not being any china to throw, of course), Major crept between their warty legs and had a look at what was in the cage. Rodney had not been wrong. The cat that sat in there was not black at all. It seemed to be every other colour a cat can be except black. It had bits of brown, bits of tabby, bits of white, bits of tortoiseshell, all mixed up. It had very, very, very long hair and the hugest eyes you've ever seen. Its whiskers were so long they drooped under their own weight, and strangest of all, the cat in the cage had massively long hair protruding from its ears and even from between its toes.

'Hello,' said Major. 'You're not black.'

'You're not so 'ot yourself, fatboy,' said the cat in the cage. 'My name's Minnie. What's your name then, eh?'

'Major,' said Major.

'Major?!' said Minnie. 'Major what? Major International Disaster Zone? Major Calamity? Major Health Warning? Major Look Major Stare Major Cut the Barber's Hair? **Ah ah ah ah ah ah.**'

After a while Major realised the cat in the cage was laughing. She didn't have the most pleasant of voices when she was speaking but this laugh, well. Most people laugh 'Ha ha ha', but Minnie most definitely laughed with an 'Ah ah ah' which was very annoying and surprisingly difficult to type. Now, as we have often said, Major was a dude. He was (apart from when grumpy) an easy-going cat. He was most definitely not a snob. At least not until now.

'How long you been in 'ere then, darl?' said Minnie, after she'd stopped laughing at her own jokes.

'Less than a week,' said Major.

'Aw, not long then, eh?'

'No. But longer than you.'

Minnie looked him up and down with a curl on her whiskers that could best be described as, well you decide:

'Aw, what, you going to be the big boss cat then?' she said. 'What you going to do, sit on me? Major Headache that would be. Major Headache! Major Pain in the Furball! Major Do It Despite Yasself! **Ah ah ah ah ah ah**.'

'Look, lady,' said Major. 'Just keep out of my way, alright?'

And he strolled back to the sofa to watch Janice and Rodney wrestling on the floor.

Well. If there was one thing Minnie did for the rest of the night, it was not keep out of Major's way.

'Wanna fight?' she said, soon after a very bruised Rodney had let her out of her cage.

'No, man,' said Major. 'I'm happy chilling just now.'

'Gawn,' she said. 'Gawn! Let's fight. **Puddum up, puddum up!**'

'Thanks but—ow!' said Major as Minnie gave him a surprisingly powerful blow to the ear. Then '**Ow**', he said again as Minnie sat up on her hind legs and started jabbing him like he was a boxing ball. After six jabs he'd had enough. He turned and kicked her hard with his back legs, then quickly turned again and pinned her to the ground. 'I said, leave me—'

'Aaaaagh,' screamed Janice in a high-pitched wail,

not unlike Lady Gaga in a blender. 'You nasty, awful brute of a cat. Leave my miniature fur-baby alone.'

Before Major could protect himself, Janice had him by the scruff of the neck and had thrown him onto the sofa in a most humiliating manner. Major licked his foot to show Janice what he thought of her, but she wasn't watching. She had her face buried deep in Minnie, whom she had gathered up and was holding like a baby.

'Was that big, nasty brute terrorising my baby, baby ball of fluffkins?' she said to Minnie's stomach. 'Do you need some protection from the ugly, fat, ginger nastyboy?'

Minnie somehow managed to ignore the fact that Janice was burying her face in her stomach. She just turned her head slowly in Major's direction and gave him a clear and cheeky wink.

Major's evening didn't get much better after that. There is a golden rule amongst cats that you never— never!—disturb another cat in the litter tray. But it was a golden rule Minnie didn't seem to know. Major was minding his own business in the bathroom and feeling pretty down in the dumps when **DOOF**! a golf ball hit him on the back of the head.

'Fore!' shouted Minnie, and came running over. 'You nearly finished or what?'

'Hey!' said Major. 'Can't you see when a tom's busy? Give me a minute.'

But even a mini-minute was many a minute too many for Minnie. Poor Major had to suffer the golf ball being thrown at him twice more before he'd finished his business. He even gave up on burying it. Oh, the indignity.

But the worst was yet to come. 'Din-dins!' shouted Janice in a high tinkling voice that she thought appealed to cats. 'Dinny-din din-dins.'

'Gorgonzola,' thought Major. 'I can't believe Ginger would ever have come here on her own accord. I wonder if . . .' But then he smelled cat food and thought nothing but 'Yummy **yummy** yummy.'

He watched patiently as Janice walked into the living-room and put down a saucer for Minnie. Then he watched patiently as she walked back into the kitchen and put down a saucer for him. Like I said, he was a dude. He wasn't one of those whiny cats that makes an absolute fool of itself every time it thinks it's going to get fed. No cheap miaowing for Major—he saved his words for when they were needed. Man. Well, dinner tonight was 'chicken with whole lobster pieces', his absolute favourite. But no sooner had he begun to eat than guess who was by his side?

'Hiya!' said Minnie. 'What'd you get?'

Major ignored her and carried on eating.

'Can I have yours? Go on, let me have yours, give us a bit, go on give us a bit, that bit there. Do you want that bit there, can I have it? Give me that bit. Why you growling?'

'Go away,' said Major. 'Eat your own dinner.'

'Didn't like it. Want yours. That bit, you want that bit, that's lobster, innit, I want it.'

Major sat back and looked at her. 'If I eat your food and give you my food, will you just shut the furball up and leave me alone?' he said.

'Cross my heart,' said Minnie. 'Yes, promise!' And without another word she sat down to eat his meal. Major sighed a big gingery sigh and walked into the living room. And what did he find there? Dandy, da dah: an empty plate! Minnie had already eaten her dinner!

'You little minx!' he growled, but by the time he was back in the kitchen his dinner was already gone too.

'**Ah ah ah ah ah**,' said Minnie. 'Fooled you. Boss cat!'

Well, boy, did this make Major grumpy. He launched himself at Minnie, who jumped out of his way and ran screaming into the living room, then up the stairs and straight into the spare room, where Janice was ironing some leftover skin she was thinking of making into a pinafore.

'**Wah**!' screamed Minnie in a deep-southern accent. '**Hayulp, hayulp**, who will hayulp me?'

Major ran after her, determined once and forever to teach her a lesson, but of course as soon as Janice saw them, she swept Minnie up into her arms and gave Major a very nasty kick.

'Rodney!' she screamed. 'Rodders, these two cats are driving me to distraction. The evil one is almost too evil, and he's going to kill my bubby babykins if we don't act soon. Let's do that commingling spell soon!'

A confused Minnie looked at Janice. 'Commingling spell?'

'Oops,' said Janice. 'Did I say "commingling spell"? Silly me. I meant "my kindling smell", my mistake. Here you go, kitty, run along. Rodney darling, we need to do my kindling smell very soon. In fact, we need to talk in private right now!'

And with that she put Minnie down, walked into the secret-upstairs-locked room, where Rodney was getting ready for a big night out, and slammed the door behind her. Then she locked it.

'What commingling what?' said Minnie to Major.

'You'll see,' said Major. 'You won't like it but you will see.'

And he walked off with his tail in the air so that from behind he looked to Minnie like a big exclamation mark on legs.

Well, all night long Minnie asked Major about the commingling spell. 'What is it? Why is it a secret? Am I involved? What are they commingling? Is it like recycling? Does it hurt? What are they doing it for?' On and on and on in that vaguely annoying accent from the wrong side of the tracks. Ooh, she was a right pain. For hours and hours and hours she miaowed at him.

But Major could be a rock when he wanted to be. He sat silently, pretending he was on a mountaintop in the Himalayas, meditating on the sound of one paw clapping. But he didn't get a wink of sleep all night, and so, come the next morning, just as Ginger and Tuck were awaiting the arrival of the first birds by the lake in the forest, he sat bleary-eyed and hungry, waiting for Rodney and Janice to come home. Poor Major didn't know it was Hallowe'en, the witches' favourite night of the year, when children are the easiest to abduct and often come with free sweets. On and on and on he waited but the day had fully dawned before he heard the elevator down the corridor opening at last and the key turning in the lock.

Then he turned to Minnie, who was still miaowing by his side and said:

'Do you want to know about the commingling spell?'

'Durrh!' said Minnie. 'You only just worked that out, did you?'

'So this is how it's going to work,' said Major. You're going to give me your breakfast. Then you're going to watch me eat it. Then you're going to watch me eat my breakfast. And then you're going to shut up and listen. Got it?'

Minnie said nothing for the first time in eight hours. Her big sticky-out hair appeared to droop very slightly at the ends.

'Oh, snot stains' she said. 'OK. But only 'cos I like you, fatboy, **ah-ah ah-ah ah-ah**.'

So both Major and his long-lost love ate well that morning. While he was tucking into his first of two full breakfasts, Ginger was sitting many miles away in the Great Dark Forest, rubbing her bellies in delight.

'Ooh, I do like a cockatoo in the morning,' she said, blowing white feathers from her mouth into the pretty woodland around her. 'Tuck, I will never say you are stupid again. That was the most marvellous display of hunting I've ever seen.'

Tuck didn't answer so she looked over at him. He was staring at her, his tongue sticking out of the side of his mouth as if he was thinking extra hard. 'Two' he said. 'Three... f— f—'

'What are you doing?' Ginger asked him.

'I'm trying to count. What's after three?'

'Four.'

'One, two, three, four...'

'Yes?'

'Ginger! You've got only four bellies!'

Ginger looked down at where she'd just been rubbing, then checked herself all over like a man who's lost his wallet. 'Oh, sweet Tabatha,' she said. 'Look at that! It must have been all the exercise and lack of food. Oh, wow.'

Tuck was confused. He'd thought Ginger loved her bellies, but now as he watched, she started strolling around with her feet right in front of each other in a very slinky way, her head stretched round so she could look at how few bellies she had.

'Why do you want to look slimmer?' he said.

'I don't,' said Ginger, sitting down suddenly. 'No reason at all. Come on, stup— stup— stupendous thingy-thing,' she said. 'It's time we got back on the trail.'

And so on they walked, deeper and deeper into the cold forest. Now, I don't know if you've been counting, but Tuck and Ginger had been walking deeper and deeper into the forest for several days ('several' is always a good number to use if you've actually lost count). There were no roads anymore, no sign of human life at all. Instead, nature was wild and unbridled, untamed and unashamed, each animal a predator and a prey. In the city there are many dangers which face a cat, but they generally come loud and announced. The forest on the other hand is full of professional hunters, bred through the generations to sneak up on and devour whatever source of protein they can find. So the cats proceeded more carefully than in preceding passages.

Every half an hour or so Ginger would stop and sniff the air behind them to see if anything was following. Or Tuck would put his head on one side and listen extra hard for the sound of breaking twigs or leaves disturbed by more than the breeze. Both would twitch their tails to extra high frequencies in the hope of picking up warning signs from the thick woodland around them. And then they would push on, into a new part of the forest with new sights, sounds and smells, where they had to learn all over again to distinguish the placid from the poisonous. No wonder they grew so tired. No wonder they were losing weight.

The deeper they walked into the forest, the more dangerous it was, until by the end of each day their nerves were more frayed than a pair of early-nineties denims. They had no way of knowing how far they had travelled, nor how far they had yet to go. Cats have an amazing sense of direction. They can find their way home from a thousand miles away, but you ask them where they are and they'll look at you blankly. Try it next time you see a cat. Walk up and ask it where it is, just see the response you get.

All Tuck and Ginger knew was that they had to press on, deeper and deeper into the forest, not even knowing when they'd passed the midpoint. They survived on whatever birds and small rodents they could find, resorting on some days to dragonflies and even the odd cockroach. They lapped at tiny forest pools or at water gathered in the broad leaves of the strange plants they found.

They rose at dawn and travelled all day, noticing how the sun got up later and lazier as autumn, season of mists and mellow fruitfulness, replaced summer in the forest. Each morning low and pale sunrays cut through the trees and cast their shadows long and eerie onto the forest floor before the sun rose above the canopy. Evening came earlier and each time cooler, and yet the cats were no less weary for the shortness of the days. They slept right through the night, curled up in a hollow tree log or under a thick bush. They thought they had less to fear that way, still and quiet in the night whilst all the hunters were about. Hidden and safe. How wrong they were.

These same days passed no less stressfully for Major. Thankfully, Rodney and Janice proved as slack about commingling Major and Minnie as about everything else. But it took Major all of this borrowed time (and all of his vast reserves of patience) to convince Minnie of what the Burringos had in mind for them. It was only when he persuaded Minnie to do her own research that she finally understood the truth. And not a moment too soon.

'No!' said Minnie, staring at the Burringos' search history on the computer screen.

'That's what I've been trying to tell you,' said Major. 'That's what they've got planned. And look at this."

He jumped down to the sofa and nuzzled his nose behind one of the cushions until it fell to the floor. There lay a copy of *Witch!* magazine open to the article on how to mix two cats into one.

'That's horrible,' said Minnie. 'I can't believe you didn't tell me. Except, well, it's horrible for me. It's great for you. I bet you're feeling really smug right now, aren't you? No wonder you don't worry about your weight.'

'What?' said Major. 'Why is it good for me?'

'Well, you get to have a beautiful new look, this stunning body of mine, all my glorious multiracial hair. Fat gingeriness will be a thing of the past. All I get is to die.'

'I am not fat.'

'You're not exactly Robert Catterson are you?'

'Listen to me, sister. You're not exactly Katie Purry yourself.'

They looked at each other until Minnie walked away and sat in the corner.

'I don't want to die,' she said quietly after a while. 'I'm not ready. Do you know how much planning it took me to get out of that dog home? I bribed the volunteers to get me a cage next to the office so I knew when people were coming in. I fed laxatives to every black cat in the building so they were all on the litter tray the day Janice came to visit. I did my best little cutesy act so I knew she'd pick me. And it all worked, it all worked, and now . . . now I'm going to die.'

Major could see Minnie was struggling to keep things together. Her entire being drooped. Then tiny tremors started at the ends of her unfeasibly long, but now very droopy ear hair, and worked their way to the very end of her big, fluffy drooping tail. There were no tears, but her hair quivered in a way that showed the full range of emotions from A to X and then to Z. There was no reason to ask why.

'Lady dude,' said Major. 'Don't stress, it'll be alright. Maybe we'll escape.'

'Really?' said Minnie in a quiet voice.

'Er, yeah, sure we will.'

'Oh great!' said Minnie, her tremors disappearing and all her hairs springing up again like an electrocuted pom-pom. 'What's the plan?'

'Er, still working on that,' said Major. 'Any ideas?'

'Ideas?' said Minnie. 'Ideas, darl! Ideas is my middle name. Don't you worry, fatboy. I'm going to get us out of here.'

'I thought you were distraught and upset and looking to me for support,' said Major. 'Where's the character consistency in you being upbeat all of a sudden?'

'I admit it,' said Minnie. 'I'm fickle. And maybe a little manic. I think it's because of my mixed heritage.'

'I imagine,' said Major, 'you're about to tell me all about it.'

'You see, I'm actually quite multiracial. On my mother's side I'm a quarter tabby, one-eighth Siamese, one-eighth blue Persian, one-sixteenth ginger, one-sixteenth white, one-eighth black, one-eighth tortoiseshell, and one-eighth Mexican.'

'And on your father's side?'

Minnie looked embarrassed. 'We're not too sure

about that,' she said hurriedly. 'But the point is I'm as cosmopolitan as a cocktail.'

'That's one word for it,' thought Major, but he didn't say anything. He had the strangest feeling he was better off with Minnie as a friend than as an enemy.

That night when the witches got up, Major and Minnie tried to act normally. They glowered at each other from across the room and ate their respective dinners in silence. Then they pretended, one after the other, to go upstairs. In reality, they sat on the bottom stair and listened to the conversation in the living room. Now, as I'm sure you know, secretly listening in on adult conversation is frequently a disappointment. Your parents rarely spend time talking about you and what you're getting for Christmas or how much they love you more than your siblings. Instead they just talk about boring things like bills and the neighbours and hygiene. Well, the same was true that night with the witches.

At least it was at first. Janice complained that she couldn't find her ball of wool, and Rodney spent so long lighting the fire that Janice threw a knitting needle at him. It stuck in his bottom, and when he stood up in shock, he banged the back of his head on the mantelpiece. He was already in a foul mood from not being able to find the firelighters, and a horrible row ensued. Unfortunately, it was over quickly, and far too soon the two witches were making up on the sofa.

'Janice darling,' said Rodney between kisses. 'Are you sure you want an evil Fluffball and not a black

Purrari? I'm keen to get you whatever you want, but it does seem like a big change of heart.'

'Oh, Roddy Boddy Bumkins,' the cats heard Janice say. 'Purraris are so tacky. And my fluffy miniature furball baby is so cute that all the other witches will be so jealous. Big brands are dead, individual is in now. Yes, yes, yes, that's what I want, give it to me, you bad boy!'

'Then tomorrow night, Janice Burringo, tomorrow night that is what you'll get. We'll give those two furbags extra dinner with sedatives, and as soon as they're sleeping we'll commingle them. But for tonight, let's go out witching. Let's catch some kids, cut them into cubes, and crisp them.'

'Oh, Rodders, how romantic.'

'Anything for you, Janice dear.'

And lots more of that cruddy slushy stuff which I'm sure you really don't want to hear about. I mean, eugh, frankly. Get a broom. Well, you can imagine the impact of hearing that conversation on our two not Tuck-and-Ginger cats. They were horrified. Major, of course, was also slightly smug that the witches had so promptly proven to Minnie what he'd been trying to tell her for a while now, but Major, being a dude, didn't think only of himself. He thought also of poor Minnie. She was, after all, supposed to be an ally now, so he put his arm around her in comfort.

''**Ere!**' she squeaked. 'Get your filfy paws off me, you dirty old tom. I've got to get busy. And if you've got nothing better to do, you can give me an 'and.'

'Busy?' said Major. 'Busy doing what exactly?'

Minnie looked at him as if he was the stupidest cat she'd ever met. 'Implementing escape plans,' she said. '**Whachoofink**?'

A REALLY, REALLY DANGEROUS BIT

Tuck was cold and tired and hungry. It seemed to him all he'd done since leaving the Burringos' apartment was walk and walk and walk. Admittedly, Ginger had taught him how to play Snap, and Tick, and how to snap at tics. But there had been no mention of any mushroom sauce since the cats in the barn had laughed at him. And now here he was in the cold and the dark, the night definitely colder than any before, and guess what the plan was for the next day? More walking.

Tuck stretched out as quietly as he could, not wanting to wake Ginger. They had made their bed on a little hillside, on a ledge beneath a big sticking-out rock. It had been warm when they'd fallen asleep, but now it was freezing. Tuck felt like someone had pressed a big slab of cold meat next to him and its chill had entered his bones. He closed his eyes, heard Ginger making a little whimpering noise in her sleep, and let his thoughts wander into the beginnings of a dream. But could he sleep? Could he buffalo. He was a night cat after all, genetically designed to hunt in the dark no matter how tired he was.

But also, something was wrong, Tuck thought, and so he opened one yellow eye. Had he heard a mouse rustling around? Should he invite it over for a game of tick? No.

But he had heard something strange. Something not quite right. Something like a whimper from a cat who never whimpered. He opened both eyes.

'Ginger,' he said quietly.

Again, Tuck heard a tiny whimper from behind him. Not nearly loud enough to be Ginger but with clear ginger accents. Suddenly he was scared. So scared he could hardly bear to turn around. What if, what if—

Tuck made himself turn, and what he saw there was far worse than anything he had what-iffed about. For all he could see of Ginger was half an eye, one ear, and most of her tail. The rest of her was completely wrapped in a huge yellow snake.

'Aaagh!' yowled Tuck. And then, in case it helped, 'Aaagh!' again.

'**Mmmf**,' said Ginger.

'What?'

'Ummfing, well, do smmfing!'

'What?'

'G'day,' said the snake, whose head suddenly appeared from where it had been burrowing under itself. 'Don't mind me.'

'I do mind you,' said Tuck. 'You're squashing my friend.'

'Tho?' said the snake, who had a rather unfortunate lisp.

'I think you're hurting her.'

'Tho?'

'It's horrible. You wouldn't like it if someone hurt you.'

'Tho?' said the snake again, lingering on the 's' with a languid hiss which would have been more subtly disturbing were it not for the lisp.

'You're going to kill her!' said Tuck.

Can you guess what the snake said? It's not rocket salad. I'm sure you can work it out. For the snake had discovered the most powerful word in the English language. He said:

'Tho?'

Well, Tuck had had quite enough of that. This hideous hissing and lisping was most miffing, and he felt himself getting highly hysterical. 'Leave her alone!' he yowled. He bared his teeth and the claws of his front two paws. He brushed himself up so he looked like a badly backcombed banshee and spat and screeched at the snake. And the snake just looked at him and licked his lips.

'You're nektht,' he thed. 'But do thut up until then, you thtoopid thilly thing.'

Well, we all know Tuck didn't like being called stupid. Or thtoopid, come to that. He jumped onto the snake and sank his claws in. He bit at its leathery yellow skin. He scrabbed and scratched and scored its scales, he screeched and scolded and called it a scallywag, but all to no avail. The snake merely squeezed Ginger a little harder than before. She gave the tiniest of whimpers, as if there was no air in her lungs for anything more than that. 'F,' she said. And that was it—she couldn't even manage a full 'Mmf'.

Tuck yelled, 'Hang on, Ginger!' and with a massive yowl and a quicker-than-the-human-eye double-twist-turn he jumped onto the snake's head. Thinking nothing of the danger to himself (and unaware that snakes that squeeze generally aren't poisonous anyway) he ignored its scary teeth and sank his own scarier teeth into one of its eyes. **Blurgh**! Blood and eye bits shot everywhere, including into Tuck's mouth, which unfortunately gave him a taste for snake's eye-bits, which he never lost and of course rarely had the opportunity to indulge very often after that.

'Hitthing hell!' screamed the snake, and moved every muscle in its horrible long body. It thrashed and lashed and bashed and crashed and smashed around, biting wildly into the air and beating its tail. But Tuck had dashed around to its blind side and was now pulling Ginger away and off the ledge where they'd made their bed, until the two of them tumbled down through the leaves and twigs of the steep slope.

'I'll get you, you hideouth puthy catth!' thcreamed the thnake. 'I'll thearch for you for the retht of my dayth.'

On and on the cats tumbled, bump bumpedy bump, head over rump, over dead bark and through leaf litter, through old spider's webs and fragile ferns until at last they found themselves at the bottom of a dark and damp hollow. Tuck lay panting until he felt well enough to sit up and pull wild webs from his whiskers. Ginger just lay there. She was breathing, that much was clear, but when Tuck asked her how she was, she merely held up her front feet to him. The message was clear: pause. So he sat there in silence and listened as his own breath slowed, and Ginger's breaths grew full and normal again, and the distant threats of the snake continued to rain down on them.

'You thcoundrelth! If I ever thee you again, you're cuthtard! You're muthtard! You're totally buthted!'

At last Ginger sat up and sniffed the air around her.

'We should go,' she said.

'We could rest a while longer if you need to,' said Tuck.

Ginger shook her head. 'It's never a good idea to rest when there's a one-eyed snake after you,' she said wisely. 'Come on, let's get going.'

And so on they walked, picking their way around the mossy rocks and muddy puddles of the creek bed that ran through this part of the forest. Steep and heavily wooded slopes ran up on either side of them, damp shadows in every direction, and the two cats wondered what strange part of the forest they now found themselves in.

'Push,' said Minnie.

'I am pushing,' said Major. 'Turn!'

'I'm trying,' said Minnie. 'But it won't turn unless you push.'

Well, I don't know if you've ever seen two pussycats trying to open a bottle of bleach, but it isn't easy. And with many other cats it would have led to a catfight. Next time you see a pair of cats chasing each other along a corridor or flailing in a fury of flying fur, have a good sniff in the air to see if you can smell bleach. If you can't, well, there you go. They obviously got into a fight because they couldn't open the bottle.

But Minnie and Major didn't fight. You see, Major had come to the realisation that he'd got off on the wrong paw with Minnie. His tactics had been Tic Tacs, his strategy a strudel. He'd tried to be boss cat when, as you will no doubt learn in life, people generally respond better when pulled rather than pushed. And cats are no different.

So, as Minnie sat on the stairs and told him her canny plans of escape, Major decided to put his ego to one side. Being something of a dude, this was easy for him. He didn't need to behave like the boss to feel like the boss because beyond all doubt he was the boss. And if Minnie didn't see it that way, it was her dross loss. So Major sat and listened and appraised and at the end of her extensive, exhaustive, and expert explanation of explosions and escape, he simply said, 'Yeah, sure, man. Just tell me what I need to do.'

Well, if there was one thing Minnie was very good at (apart from being annoying, getting people into trouble, picking locks, disturbing the peace, waking people up, and looking cute), it was telling cats what to do. All night long she had Major bending coat hangers and shredding paper, catching flies and sawing wood, pulling threads from the nylon bathmat, and even weeing into a small saucer. And now she had him trying to open a bottle of bleach.

'Push!' she said again. 'Come on, fatboy, use that weight of yours!'

Major sat back from the huge bleach bottle and gave her a flat-eyed look.

'Excuse me,' he said. 'Dude?'

'Sorry,' said Minnie. Then she sat in silence for a

minute, clearly as deep in thought as she ever got. 'I know!' she said suddenly. 'Let's try another approach. Let's bite froo the plastic!'

'OK, man,' said Major, who was not a little exhausted after all the night's efforts. 'Go for it.'

'Oh, but I couldn't,' said Minnie, fluttering her huge false eyelashes. 'I'm just a poor little female cat with weak jaws and blunt little toothypegs, innit? I need a big masculine man cat with muscly mandibles to do it for me. Know what I mean?'

Well, I'm not sure I can quite convey the gingeriness of the sigh that greeted that little performance. No man likes a princess and no Major does either. But he stood up and put his mouth around what looked like the weakest part of the bottle. He squeezed his jaws and grunted and grinded and bit harder and harder until 'Eugh!' he said. 'Eugh, eugh, eugh!'

He spat onto the kitchen counter. 'I've got bleach on my teeth!' he said.

'Oh, but they do so look sparkly white, **ah ah ah ah ah**,' laughed Minnie. 'Come on. It's baking soda next. Maybe you can brush them too. **Ah ah ah ah**.'

A couple of hours later, when the Burringos arrived home from their sandal-lit dinner, what did they find in the apartment? A mess of half-spilled bomb ingredients strewn across the kitchen? A cleverly constructed contraption combining combustibles and complicated crosswires? **Bony-baloney, no!** They found nothing but two innocent-looking cats hungry for their breakfast and looking like they'd just woken up.

'Aw, look at them, I think they're beginning to get along,' said Janice, through a full, foul, and filling-filled yawn.

'Whatevs,' said Rodney. 'There'll be getting along a lot better tomorrow night when they're sharing the same body.'

'Mwah ha ha ha,' cackled Janice, giddy already at the idea of her own evil furball companion.

The two cats looked at them, dumbly wondering why the witches had forgotten they could understand every word they said.

'They're probably drunk,' thought Major.

'Too right,' thought Minnie.

And too right they were indeed. For after the restaurant Janice and Rodney had gone to a belated Hallowe'en party. Hallowe'en had fallen on a Tuesday that year, and so Janice and Rodney had had to wait for the weekend before any parties came along. Now, witches, like everyone else apart from dudes, are not very patient at the best of times, so by the time the party came along, it was a rambunctious and raucous affair where the best night of the year was feted and celebrated until all were belatedly sated.

The hosts, Beleasha and Barry Beacon from Birmingham, were old friends of Rodney's from his college days, and, boy, did they know how to throw a party. They served little boys' bits on cocktail sticks with pieces of pineapple, watermelon wrapped in still-warm tongue, and prawn salad with all the poo-tubes left in. To drink there was a choice of beers: liquid-gout stout, dirt-from-under-the-Aga lager and stale ale. There were a few white wines (wee-sling, soap-onion blanc, and chardonnay) and of course a Hungarian bull's blood.

But it was the cocktails that were the undoing of Janice and Rodney. After a few too many shots of ToKillHer, they knocked back the Caipirranhas like there was no price to be paid. Trust me, folks—there is always a price to be paid. My suggestion is to avoid alcohol completely until you're about twenty-five and you've let everyone else learn the lessons for you. Then you can proceed straight to smug without passing go or collecting two hundred dollars. Oh, how wise. Oh, how sensible. Oh, how Rod 'n' Jan should have paid heed to such words.

But they didn't. At about three o'clock in the morning, Beleasha Beacon had to ask them to leave the party for vomiting on everyone's cloaks, which were piled in a corner. Janice of course refused. She shed she wash having sush a good time woy should she do anything that fatsho told her to do. Then a rather embarrassing fight broke out, which ended up with Janice and Rodney being thrown out on their bus passes. Fat lot of good a bus pass is when it's too late to get a bus! Of course, they couldn't get a taxi to stop for them, what with the state they were in, and they were far too drunk to ride home on their broomsticks. So they had to walk all the way. Then, halfway home, it started raining, and the first of winter's cold winds started to blow. So now they arrived home sodden, cold, and not in the most rational of dispositions. Hence them talking to the cats as if they couldn't understand. And hence Major smiling quietly to himself, thinking how deeply they would sleep all day.

'Noight noight, puddycatsh,' said Janice as Rodney pushed her up the stairs.

'Lawks and lemmings,' said Minnie, once the secret-upstairs-locked room door had closed on Janice's off-key warbling. ''Ow common!'

Major looked at her and said nothing.

Meanwhile, back in the forest, that same cold wintry wind had also brought a rainstorm. Tuck and Ginger had walked in the dark down the creek bed to a strange flood plain of willowy trees with well, plane trees and willows, flat flat-bits and grassy grass. The canopy above was sparse now, but above it the sky had grown so thick with clouds that the night was darker than in even the deepest part of the forest. There were no stars or moon tonight, just ominous black clouds. Neither cat needed to say that rain was on the way—they could smell it in the breeze. And not piddly-tiddly spitty little pitter-patter rain either. This was going to be a big-drop drama.

Ginger was still weak from her cuddle with the python, and Tuck was bored, bored, bored of walking, and both of them were exhausted. But they knew they had to get under thicker cover ASAP, so on they pressed in the vague hope they would find something up ahead. All too soon they heard a rumble in the distance, and soon after that they saw a flash in the not-very-far-off sky. Then, sooner than either of them had expected, huge great drops of rain began to hit the ground around them. Drops so huge that they threw up tiny explosions of dirt as they landed. Still the cats pressed on, for what else could they do? It wasn't two minutes before they were both soaked to the skin. Tuck felt as miserable as he ever had done, but he decided to tough it out just to show how big and brave he was.

'I want to go home!' he said after five minutes. 'I don't like it here. It's scary, and there's strange animals, and it's cold, and I miss cat food and the sofa and the television, and I'm hungry and tired, and . . . and . . . what's that?'

Ginger had stopped when Tuck had started yowling. She sat looking at him, wondering how best to motivate him out of this prissy sissy hissy fit. But halfway through she'd seen something behind him, which had taken her concentration away from everything he was saying.

'What?' she said.

'What's that?' said Tuck again. 'What's that thing?'

'Hang on,' she said. 'What's that? It's like a light behind you.'

'Yes!' said Tuck. 'Behind you too. It's like a little window.'

And Tuck stood, his tears washed away by the torrential rain, and crept cautiously over to what he had seen. It was half-buried in the ground beneath a thick tuft of grass. Ginger was still a little nervy after the evening she'd had, so she followed Tuck closely rather than investigate the little light she'd first seen. But as she did so, she saw there were other faint lights here and there in the grass, near and farther away.

'It's a tunnel!' said Tuck. 'A tunnel with a little light at the end! Let's shelter in here.'

'No!' said Ginger. 'It might be a foxhole.'

At this Tuck froze. He'd not forgotten what foxes like to eat. Ginger came and stood beside him and sniffed at the mouth of the tunnel. It didn't smell like a fox. It smelled more like . . .

'Oh, hello!' said a rather posh voice suddenly. 'Lord, what weather we're having!'

Both cats jumped off all four paws, and their hair stood up as if they'd been electrocuted. They spun around and saw, right behind them where they hadn't noticed it before, another opening to a tunnel. In it stood a dapper little rabbit in a tweed waistcoat and smoking a pipe.

'How do you do?' said the rabbit.

'Are you, are you, are you a fox?' said Tuck.

'How very, very rude,' said the rabbit. 'No, I am most certainly not. Really!'

'Sorry,' said Ginger. 'My friend is a housecat—he doesn't know much about animals. He hates foxes, that's why he asked.'

'Oh,' said the rabbit, visibly relaxing. 'Well, any chap that hates a fox can't be all bad, I suppose. How d'you do. My name is Bartholomew P. Wilkins.'

'I'm Ginger,' said Ginger. 'And this is Tuck.'

'Devil of a night for it,' said the rabbit.

'Yes,' said Tuck. 'We're looking for somewhere to shelter. Are there any thicker trees near here?'

'Trees, old boy? On a night like tonight?' said the rabbit. 'Wouldn't hear of it. Come on in, I insist. I feed enough bally mouths in this household every night. I'm sure another two won't hurt. Come on, come on, I'll leave you there to have a good shake and see if I can find each of you a spare jacket.'

And with that he disappeared down the tunnel and around the corner.

'Jacket?' said Tuck as Ginger gave herself a good shake and then licked off the worst of the residual raindrops.

'Oh yes,' said Ginger. 'Rabbits are very proper, you know. They always dress for dinner. Just be careful what you say—they've got this real thing about etiquette.'

'Rabbits?' said Tuck. 'Are you sure?'

Ginger hissed at him as she could hear Mr Wilkins scampering back up the corridor.

Most of the lights, it turned out, were coming from the Wilkinses' dining room. It was filled with tiny fireflies, whose humming was the only sound as Mrs M Ginger (formerly of Heatherington Hall) and Mr Spencer Tuck, Esquire, were introduced.

'**Ooh, helloo**,' said Mrs Wilkins in a gorgeous smoky voice as she extended a furry paw. '**How do you dooo**?' Tuck shook Mrs Wilkins's paw, while Ginger stood behind him and pushed his head down until it was just above Mrs Wilkins's tiny engagement ring.

'Ooh, helloo,' said Ginger. 'Hi do ye do. It's so awfully kind of you to shelter us from the rain like this.'

'Er . . . what she said,' said Tuck, who was a little too scared to say anything else.

The cats were then introduced to the Wilkinses' twenty-six children, who stood and introduced themselves in turn. Their names were Annabel, Bartholemew Jnr, Camilla, Diana, Edward, Frederick, Giles, Hubert, India, Jemima, Katharine, Lucinda, Margaret, Nigella, Oscar, Primrose, Quentin, Rupert, St John, Tamara, Ursula, Virginia, William, Xaviera, Yolanda, and Zara.

'Goodness,' said Tuck. 'What an awful lot of—' but Ginger elbowed him hard in the ribs, so he just said, 'lovely names', and no one will ever know what he was originally going to say. An awkward silence followed, until the very smallest of the Wilkins children, baby Zara, who was barely more than a ball of fluff, pointed at Ginger and asked loudly, 'Why's the saggy moggie soggy, Mommie?' Well! Poor Mrs Wilkins blushed bright red, but Ginger pretended not to hear and commented on how charming her curtains were.

'We were about to eat,' said Mrs Wilkins. 'Would you join us?'

'Oh, we couldn't possibly,' said Ginger, much to Tuck's dismay. He looked at her with wide yellow eyes and wondered if her jacket was too tight. Not only was she talking in a very strange way (her mouth made as small as possible and her vowels clipped and snipped and chipped into shape), now she was refusing dinner.

'**Oh, dooo**!' said Mrs Wilkins. '**I simply insist**.'

'Honestly, we couldn't impose,' said Ginger.

'Bally nonsense!' barked Mr Wilkins from the other end of the table. 'I won't hear another word of it. Sit down and grab yourselves a toastie.'

Well, poor old Tuck thought a plate had never moved around a table so slowly. He was already salivating from the sight of so many tiny fluffy bunnies in a confined space. He knew whatever else he did, he mustn't mention a game of tick or something very unfortunate might happen. And although he didn't know how to speak in a funny way and had never worn a jacket for dinner before, he knew it was probably bad form to eat a family that had taken you in from a cold and stormy night. But, oh, he wished those plates of food would be passed around quicker.

They had started in front of him, a huge plate of cheese toasted sandwiches on one and an even huger plate of tomato toasted sandwiches on the other. As Tuck watched, one plate went one way round the table, one went the other. It was only after a good five minutes, and when each plate was significantly lighter than it had started out, that he saw them both arriving back in front of him again.

'Mr Tuck, my dear,' said Mrs Wilkins kindly. 'Do help yourself. Would you like a cheese toastie or a tomato toastie? Or one of each?'

'Ooh, both please!' said Tuck, somewhat excitedly after such a long wait. 'I really love mixing my toasties!'

A horrible hush descended upon the dining room. Every one of the little Wilkins bunnies turned at Tuck with a horrified expression, apart from little Zara, who sat giggling in the corner with a paw over her mouth. Mrs Wilkins looked horrified, and Mr Wilkins muttered, 'Bad taste, bad form' under his breath. Even the fireflies hushed their buzzing for a while, and the light in the room faded as if during a power shortage. Tuck had no idea what he'd done and maybe you don't know either? If not, go and ask an adult why you should never say to a rabbit 'I love mixing my toasties' and you might learn something. Adults do have some uses, after all. Unfortunately for Tuck, there was no one for him to ask.

'Toasties,' said Ginger, 'are what the French call toasted sandwiches, I believe. Is that right, Mr Tuck?'

Tuck sat silently and stared at Ginger, his eyes huge and yellow and uncertain. He watched her nod very slowly and eventually stuttered out, 'Y-y-yes?'

'Yes. You see, Mr Tuck and I summered in Paris this year,' Ginger continued, smiling benevolently at the crowded table, 'and the dear French always talk about mixing their toasted sandwiches. It's a funny expression although—'

'Indeed!' said Mrs Wilkins, brightening slightly and allowing Ginger to engage her in a witty discussion on the price of carrots. Tuck was so terrified he didn't speak another word all evening. He let the children talk instead, listening carefully to their conversations about grass and the forest and the weather, and wondering what on earth he had done wrong.

Unfortunately, he never got to ask Ginger that night (their rooms were in separate wings of the burrow), and the next morning he forgot. By the time he remembered again, there was a far more important question that needed answering.

A BIT OF
BLOOD AND GUTS

The next day the Burringos' apartment was silent but for the sound of Rodney and Janice's drunken snoring. And I hope you like big buts because that was a HUGE one. The apartment wasn't silent at all. It was rollicking and rolling and trembling and tremoring to the sounds of their snoring.

'It's a flippin' urfquake!' screamed Minnie when it first started. 'It's de end offer wurld! Gawd, listen to them 'ooters gowing! **Ah ah ah ah ah ah ah**!'

She was clearly excited. She and Major had spent all night preparing for their prison break, and now she was to have her big moment. Her 'Big Bang' as she'd referred to it seventeen times that night. Now there was nothing to do but wait. Wait for the Burringos to fall asleep (that bit was easy) and then wait some more until she and Major could hear someone in the corridor calling the lift. That bit wasn't so easy, at least it wasn't for Minnie.

'Bleeding 'eck' she said. 'What's keeping 'em? 'Ow many people is there on this floor?'

'Six apartments,' said Major, who had counted the doors on the way in despite his scruff-held state. 'Patience, Minnie-man, They generally go out after breakfast.'

But telling Minnie to be patient was like telling a patient to feel better. Not gonna happen.

'Dude,' said Major, 'why don't you double-check all the arrangements while I get a bit of shut-eye. I'm really tired.'

And with that he curled up on the arm of the sofa and lay the end of his tail over his nose. But in reality he was too nervous to sleep. He was worried about all the things that could go wrong and how angry the witches would be with him and Minnie if they did. So Major lay there with his eyes wide open, chanting an om under his breath whilst he watched Minnie check the arrangements. Which basically meant sniffing all along the wool she'd stolen from Janice's knitting basket the night before.

While Major was looking for baking powder, she'd unravelled it and rubbed Rodney's missing firelighter along it a hundred and twenty times until she'd created a perfect fuse wire. One end of it was now connected to the gas hob in the kitchen, and the other lay in a two-litre bottle of explosive liquid just inside the front door. Try as hard as they could the cats had not been able to disable the sprinkler system in the flat so they had opened all the umbrellas they could find over the carpet near the door. Here lay the rest of the firelighters surrounded by a strange assortment of cooking oils.

'I'm worried about the sprinklers,' said Minnie, who could see Major was still awake. 'What if dey put the fire out straightaway, eh? Who has a sprinkler system in their 'ouse anyway?'

'Most witches,' said Major tiredly through the end of his tail. 'It's a cultural thing. They've got this big thing about fire. People used to burn witches.'

'Lack of wood?' said Minnie.

'Who knows?' said Major.

Then they both heard a noise in the corridor. It was the little old lady next door (the same little old lady who by not-that-big-a-coincidence-really had helped Tuck and Ginger's escape). She had opened the front door to her apartment, closed it behind her, and was now making her way towards the lift. Major stood bolt upright. He and Minnie looked at each other, and then they both ran to the kitchen.

Lighting the stovetop was relatively easy. They simply had to push and turn at the same time. They'd practised it a hundred times on the bleach bottle, but now their nerves got in the way. Major chose the biggest knob, leant on it hard and twisted. But he slipped, a thin veil of sweat on the pads of his paws.

'Hurry,' said Minnie. 'We'll miss the lift!'

Major tried again, and again he failed to light the stove. He sat back, closed his eyes, and let out an especially deep and gingery sigh. 'Be the flame,' he said to himself. He leant on the knob once more, and it was as if it turned itself. Click, click, click went the ignition, and **boof!** The flames around the biggest element sprang to life.

'Now we're cooking wiv gas,' said Minnie.

The wool that was tied around the stovetop caught the flame immediately, and the cats watched eagerly as the little flicker of fire burnt along its length. Within ten seconds it had reached the floor, and within another thirty it had reached the kitchen door.

'Eeez gonna make beeg bang,' said Minnie in her best Mexican accent.

But she spoke too soon. She and Major sat with their paws in their ears, but a minute later they were still there and nothing had made beeg bang at all.

'No,' said Minnie. 'No! What's wrong?'

And she jumped down to see what could have happened.

'No!' said Major. 'Wait!'

But it was too late. Minnie stepped outside of the kitchen door just as the massive explosion rocked not only the apartment but the entire apartment building. *BO* . . . Oh, I'll run out of vowels if I even try to describe it. It was big, got it? No, bigger than that. Bigger. Bit bigger. No, much bigger. Bit bigger still. OK, that's it. Really, really big. **KERRBOOOO OOOOOOOOOOOOOOOOOOOOOOOO OOOOOOOOOOOOOOOOOOOOOOOO OM**. Sorry, I couldn't resist.

'Minnie!' shouted Major.

He jumped down from what was left of the kitchen work surface and ran out into the hall. Where there had once been a front door was a massive gaping hole. What was left of the door was halfway down the corridor towards the elevator, leaning against the wall at an angle and burning in bright yellow flames. Beyond it stood a somewhat braised little old lady, soot all over her face, her hair in the air like Einstein's, and her hat hanging down under her chin. Inside the apartment was a scene of carnage. The sofa was smoking, the carpet inside the front door was blazing, the floorboards were warped.

And there, squashed onto the television screen like roadkill, was Minnie. Major had never seen her so still. No one had ever seen her so still.

'Minnie?' said Major, walking towards her. 'Minnie, are you . . . are you—'

Just then the elevator at the other end of the corridor went *ping*. Minnie raised her head, gave Major a massive wink and said, 'I tell you, meester. It make beeg bang! Look at me, Major, I'm on television! **Ah ah ah ah ah ah ah**! Oops, elevator!'

And with that she peeled herself off the television screen and sprang towards the front door. '**WHOOPEE WOO**!' she screeched as she jumped headlong over the burning carpet and into the smoking corridor. 'Hold that lift!'

Major ran after her and he didn't do it a moment too soon, for just then Rodney Burringo appeared at the top of the stairs. He was green and warty and had death in his eyes, not to mention one of the top ten hangovers ever recorded. He flew down the stairs, literally, stopping only when he reached the flames at the bottom. Just then the sprinkler system kicked in, and within a damp minute the flames were out.

But a damp minute was more than Major and Minnie needed. They raced past the little old lady who was (a) getting used to pairs of cats tearing out of the Burringos', and (b) in catatonic shock at the huge explosion, and into the lift. Minnie hurried to the back corner, turned, and ran full speed at Major. She sprang onto him and bounced up to the >|< button with another 'Whoopee-woo!'

But before she could press her nose to the button, Rodney Burringo came flying out of his apartment on his fastest broomstick. 'Kill!' he yelled, and pointed an evil finger at the lift.

The kill spell, which all witches have at their disposal, left his dirty fingernail and travelled down the corridor at high speed. It passed the broken and smouldering apartment door as Minnie pushed the >|< button with her nose. It passed the little old lady as the elevator doors began to close. It reached the elevator doors just after they had closed. Then it bounced off the reflection of the elevator doors and started on its journey back along the corridor just as the little old lady said, 'Oh hello, Mr Burringo. Did you—' But that was as far as she got because that is as far as the kill spell got. It hit the little old lady square in the back, and before Rodney Burringo could cover his eyes and mouth, the little old lady exploded all over the corridor. Splat. Gulp.

'What was that 'orrible noise?' said Minnie.

'No idea,' said Major. 'Let's not wait around to find out. Quick—let's go again.'

And so again Minnie hurried to the back corner, again she ran full speed at Major, who in his early years had been bottom-left in a cat pyramid touring troupe, and again she bounced off him up to the buttons. This time she hit the 'G' button, and quicker than you could say 'Goodness, I bet Tuck and Ginger wish they'd thought of that', the two cats were travelling down to the ground floor.

Talking of Tuck and Ginger, they too were once more on their way. It took a good forty-five minutes for them to say their goodbyes to the Wilkins family. It was worth it, though, as they were fed a huge breakfast, and as if that weren't enough, each of them was given a little basket full of sandwiches and chocolate eggs which were left over from Easter. Ginger told Mrs Wilkins she and Mr Wilkins really must look them up next time they were on the other side of the Great Dark Forest, and Mr Wilkins told Tuck something about rugby, which Tuck didn't understand. At last, fed and happy and struggling to carry their baskets, the two cats trotted off even further into the forest whilst the twenty-eight rabbits waved them out of sight.

Of course, as soon as they *were* out of sight, Ginger and Tuck dropped the baskets, emptied the contents onto the ground and scoffed their way through all the sandwiches and all the chocolates, although not necessarily in that order. Oh, can you imagine the purring, chomping sound they made? You can't? Try harder.

'You know,' said Ginger, picking silver paper from between her teeth. 'You can say what you like about rabbits, but they are very generous hosts. I reckon we could have stayed there another week.'

'Really?' said Tuck, his mouth still full of grass paste, crusts, and chocolate. 'Why didn't we, then?'

It was a tough question for Ginger to answer. She too was tired of walking, and the idea of sitting out the stormy season in a nice warm burrow had been tempting. Truth be told, though, she wasn't sure she could have resisted helping herself to a little baby bunny for that long. She found herself drooling and tried to think of something else.

'It's still thundering in the distance,' she said to Tuck. 'We should press on. These willows won't give us much shelter.'

And so on they pushed. Soon the ground rose up from the flat valley floor, and the willows gave way to thick pine trees bigger than even Ginger had heard of. Here the forest floor was almost bare. Plants need water and sunlight to thrive, but down here little sunlight and less rain made it through the thick pine branches overhead. There was little to see but for old pine needles and endless tree roots crissing and crossing in a spaghetti of half-buried wood. After the breezy trees and waving grass of the floodplain, it was eerily quiet. The distant rumble of thunder was the only sound.

'Maybe we should sit out the storm in here?' said Tuck.

'Maybe,' said Ginger.

But they both carried on walking, padding quietly across the carpet of pine needles. Neither of them could explain why they carried on. It wasn't as if they'd find a better shelter. But there was something about this part of the forest that felt different from any they'd found before. There was a different energy, nothing you could see or smell but something indescribable you could feel. At least, you could if you were a cat.

As Tuck and Ginger walked, they looked up occasionally into the trees, trying to work out if the storm was coming closer, but the trees were too thick to let them know. Certainly, the thunder was louder than before. It never stopped, not for a minute, and as they got higher and higher up the hill they discussed if maybe it wasn't thunder at all but a huge river or a mighty waterfall. Soon they were referring to it not as 'the thunder' but as 'the noise'. The closer they got to it the less comfortable they felt. They tracked to the left of their true path thinking maybe they could avoid it, and then they backtracked back and had a crack from the right. But no matter how far they walked to one side or the other, the noise remained in front of them.

There was no choice. They were going to have to tackle it head-on. Tuck spotted a huge fallen tree, and he jumped onto it to see what was ahead. As if from nowhere, a large wild turkey flew up in front of him, its great beating wings and squawking beak making him jump so much he almost fell back off the log. By the time he'd recovered himself, the turkey had got into the low branches of a majestic pine.

'Hee haw,' the turkey squawked. 'Can't get me now!'

'I didn't want to get you,' said Tuck. 'I've had a huge breakfast and lots of chocolate.'

'Yeah, whatever,' said the turkey. 'Go on, bet you'd like a bit of me, really. You wanna piece of me? You want that? C'mon, c'mon, show us what you've got.'

By this time Ginger too had jumped on the fallen log and was sitting next to Tuck. She gave the turkey a cool look.

'Buzz off,' she said. 'Unless . . .'

'Unless what?' said the turkey. 'You don't scare me.

You come up here and say "unless". Cats in the forest! Now I've seen it all. Bet you think I'm scared. Well, I'm not. I'm wild, man, I'm outta control. I can do what I want.'

'Unless,' said Ginger, 'you want to show us what's making all that noise? We thought it was thunder at first, but now I'm not so sure. We're going to have a look—want to come?'

The turkey opened his eyes wide and looked from Ginger to Tuck, from Tuck to Ginger, head going from side to side and from front to back all at the same time.

'You what?' he gobbled. 'You what? You don't want to go there, you can't . . . You can't make me. I won't do it, you can't force me. It's suicide, you crazy cats.'

And with that he flapped his wings and jumped up to the next branch up the pine tree. 'Suicide!' he squawked, jumping and flapping (it could hardly be called flying) up to another higher branch, and then higher and higher again until his tiny squawks of 'suicide' could hardly be heard.

'Cheeses,' said Ginger. 'What a turkey.'

Then she looked up at the tree which the turkey had climbed and said, 'Hang on, I've got an idea.'

'Is it let's go back the way we came?' said Tuck hopefully.

Ginger didn't answer him. Instead, she walked over to the tree, sank her claws into its bark, and started climbing. Tuck sat forlornly and watched her not-as-big-as-before-but-still-somewhat-sizeable bottom disappearing up into the branches.

'But there's no firemen here,' he said. 'Who's going to get us down again?'

When he got no answer, he asked the question again, in more of a yowl than a miaow, a kind of miaowl if you like. Only then did he realise that Ginger was out of earshot. He suddenly felt very alone in the eerie dark of the forest floor. 'Oh no,' he said. 'I'm going to climb a tree.'

It didn't take Tuck long to catch up to Ginger. She was an expert climber and had once led an SAS team across the Alps, but she was out of shape and no competition for Tuck's athleticism. 'Go past,' she wheezed when they were about twenty metres up. 'I need a rest. You go on.'

And so up Tuck went, all his fear of trees suddenly forgotten, climbing higher and higher, the turkey still flapping high above him. 'You wanna piece of me?' it was yelling again. 'Come and get it, you carnivore.'

Soon the view either side of the tree started to clear. Up here the branches that stuck out to the side were shorter and so the trees, thick and amongst each other down near the ground, appeared to grow further apart. The higher and higher Tuck climbed the brighter the air grew around him until suddenly, seventy metres up in the sky, the view cleared. There were no thunderclouds at all, just a huge pale blue sky. Tuck could see all the way to the horizon. Between him and it there was nothing to see but thousands and thousands of trees, a great green sea rolling in time to the breeze.

'**Oooooh**,' said Tuck. 'Wowwwww.'

When Ginger eventually caught him up he was still staring at the massive expanse of trees.

'Do we have to go all that way?' he said. 'Just the idea of it makes me tired.'

'Well,' said Ginger. 'Do you see way out there on the horizon? You see where it's uneven and little blocks of grey are standing up?'

Tuck nodded sadly. It seemed a very, very, very, very, very, very, very, very long way away.

'That's the city,' said Ginger. 'That's how far we've come already.'

'No!' said Tuck, turning to look at her so suddenly he almost lost his footing on the branch. 'No way.'

'Toadily way,' said Ginger. 'But what I'm more interested in is the other direction. What's making all that noise?'

And without another word she climbed even higher up the tree. The turkey meanwhile had reached the pine tree's very highest branch and was sitting there quietly, not knowing quite what to say. He figured if he jumped and flapped enough he'd probably get to another tree before he hit the ground, but he was too much of a turkey to try it. This thought annoyed him even more than the idea of being eaten by two cats, and he sat morosely dwelling on his place in the universe, wondering if it was possible to have a midlife crisis so shortly before his death.

But the cats weren't interested in the turkey, for they had found another view, a clearing in the branches that looked in the opposite direction from the city. There, so close it appeared to be right below them, they discovered the source of the thunderous noise. It was not a river, nor was it a waterfall. It was something far more deadly and dangerous and difficult to cross.

A BIT OF
PEACE AND QUIET,
BUT NOT FOR LONG

Where are we?' said Minnie.

'We're about two blocks north of Piddle Street,' said Major without looking up. He was washing his hind legs, trying to get out the scorch marks from where he'd jumped over the fire. The fur was all crinkly and black there, and although you or I might not have noticed it, to such a dapper dude as Major it was downright disgusting.

'No,' said Minnie. 'I mean, what is this place?'

Major was considering whether he should just nibble the charred fur or if that would leave a bald patch. It was a point for some serious consideration, and Minnie's questions were an annoying disturbance. 'What does it look like?' he said.

Minnie looked around her. They'd bombed, then pelted, then run, then trotted, then walked, and finally strolled from the inner suburbs into the city centre itself. Minnie didn't know the city very well (for reasons which may yet become clear, although I promise nothing), but Major knew every back alley and bakery. So Minnie followed without questions when he said 'Left here' or 'Right up there' or 'Between that broken bit of fence' and 'Down these steps' until she was completely and utterly lost.

Minnie and Major were in the very backest alley she'd ever been in. On all sides huge deserted tenement blocks reached up to the sky, four different back walls, each with its own style of dirty bricks, broken windows and torn curtains. They'd entered via a narrow gap between two of the buildings, picking their way under dead bicycles, past smelly milk cartons, and between pieces of newspaper that had blown in there in the seventies and never managed to blow out again.

And now they found themselves here, in a dank clearing in the concrete jungle. The sky seemed a very long way overhead. The ground floors of the buildings around them were hidden behind a ramshackle fence made of a thousand different types of wood nailed or stacked together in a very haphazard fashion. Old doors held up planks from building sites, the remains of chairs were glued to flooring timber; ancient crates and tea chests had been smashed flat and squashed against each other. It was like a museum of rubbish, all of it faded and rain-worn.

And on the ground between all of this was nothing, nothing but dust, where Major sat licking his legs and Minnie stood asking questions.

'Lord, lovely spot you've brought me to,' she said. 'It's not the 'ilton, is it? You bring all your young ladies here?'

'You never heard of the Furom?'

'Why? Is it near 'ere?'

'No,' said Major. 'You're standing in the middle of it.'

Minnie's eyes grew wide and she looked around again. Those deserted tenement blocks were the famous stands! That ramshackle fence was the ancient barrier!

'I don't believe it,' she said. ''Ere, aren't you full of 'em, eh?'

And she said several other meaningless phrases as she turned around and around whilst Major decided to nibble off a bit of the black fur on his leg to see what it looked like.

I suppose I ought to explain at this point a little about catfights. Back in 1798, when the first superleague was formed in the backstreets of Paris . . . Actually, maybe I'll come forward in time a bit. After the split of the WCFL from the WLCC and the burning of the Catisserie Générale de Paris . . . Yeah, that's a bit complicated too. Are you familiar with the UA Fur Cup? Supergrowl? Ultimate Fight Cat?

OK, how to explain this?

Imagine the most famous sports stadium in the entire world. Well, for cats that's the Furom. Just to fight there is an honour, five thousand caterwauling cats walling you in on all sides, spray and popcorn filling the air, the ancient barrier ensuring any pussy pugilists stay put and fight it out. Minnie had never thought she'd get to see the mythical place. Some said it didn't even exist, and giving directions on how to get there was banned, for the first rule of catfight is 'You don't talk about catfight'.

'Did Muhammad Alley ever fight here?' asked Minnie.

'Yup,' said Major. 'Although he was just Catsius Clay in those days.'

'What about Scratch Hindlegs, the famous southpaw?'

But before Major could answer, they both heard a

noise behind the barrier. It was a slow creaking, like an ancient door being opened, quiet at first but growing louder. Minnie shrank back from it and squeezed up tight to Major.

'Whassat then?' she squeaked. 'Oh crikey, what'll they do if they find us 'ere?'

But before Major could answer this question either, a huge pallet fell out of the barrier and crashed down onto the concrete just in front of them, throwing a cloud of dust into the air. When it cleared, there was a big black gap in the fence. Minnie blinked the dust out of her eyes and squinted into the darkness. There, to her horror, she made out the biggest cat she had ever seen. He was the size of a dog. And not some namby-pamby, scrunchy-scrawny, handbag dog either. Oh no. He was the size of a medium brown dog. He was long-haired and tabby, his huge, thick legs ending in claws, which any cat's eye could see had been sharpened. He wore a thick, gold collar encrusted with sharp, pointy diamonds. He glowered from the darkness behind the barrier with intense green eyes.

'Eek,' yowled Minnie. She stepped sideways and pointed at Major. 'It was 'is idea. I thought we was going shoppin'!'

The giant tabby looked at her ferociously and then turned his gaze upon Major, who had decided bald was better than burnt (who could disagree?) and was now nibbling away more fur.

'Oh yeah?' said the huge tabby in a thick American accent. 'And who's he when he's at home?'

At which point Major looked up from his nibbling.

Immediately the giant tabby's ferocious frown turned upside down into a smile that wouldn't have looked out of place in Cheshire.

'Major!' he said as he stepped out into the light, his huge paws throwing up more clouds of dust. He bumped his nose against Major's and rubbed his tabby side against Major's newly bald back legs.

'Dude,' said Major.

'I don't believe it,' said the gigantic tabby. 'What the smell are you doing here? I heard you and Ginger moved to the countryside. Running a pharmacy or something?'

'Farm,' said Major, who hated exaggeration.

''Scuse me?' said Minnie, who never before and never again looked as tiny as she did next to the giant cat. 'Huc-hum? Introductions, d'you mind?'

'Well, well, well,' said the tabby, looking her (not very far) up and down. 'Hello, kitty. Who's this, Major? You out on the tiles for the weekend or something?'

'This is Minnie,' said Major. 'Not what you think. Minnie, this is Oscar. Oscar De La Pawya.'

'Ooh, 'ello, big boy,' said Minnie. 'You a fighter, then? Show us your claws, go on.'

Oscar smiled awkwardly and pretended his ear needed scratching.

'Ooh, 'e's shy!' said Minnie. 'In't that sweet. Mind if I look around?'

And without waiting for an answer, she walked over the pallet that had fallen in the dust and into the tunnel entrance it had revealed. Oscar asked where Ginger was, and Major told him the whole story. Well, not the bits you've read about Ginger and Tuck because clearly he didn't know that bit. But he told him the rest.

'And you came here looking for her?' said Oscar. 'I'm sorry, buddy. She's not been here. Not that I've heard anyway.'

Which meant she hadn't been there. Nothing went on in the Furom without Oscar knowing about it. You don't keep control of a wilful whirl of wildcats without having a firm paw on every detail.

'It was a vague hope,' said Major. 'But that's not really why I came. I'm looking for Jimmy the Stink. He owes me a favour.'

'Ha. You have been away a long time. Jimmy might as well be domesticated. He came off the wrong side of a disagreement with a car. Said that when you get down to only three lives you get to thinking about your—what was the word?—legacy. You'll never guess where he is now.'

Major laughed out loud (something he rarely did) when Oscar told him where to find Jimmy. But his laugh was interrupted by an empty popcorn carton which landed heavily on top of his head. He and Oscar looked up to see Minnie sitting on the best second-floor windowsill.

'It's rabbish so far,' she cackled. 'You two pussies gonna fight each uvver, or do I 'ave to come dan there an show you 'ow it's dan? Ah ah ah ah ah ah ah ah!'

'Who did you say she was again?' said Oscar.

'I didn't,' said Major. 'Now, about Jimmy the Stink and that favour he owes me . . .'

An hour later, Major and Minnie entered a narrow alleyway that smelled of nothing but dried urine—and not all of it from cats. Halfway along, Major stopped and Minnie realised there was a large door in the wall. Before she could ask what it was, a small portion of the door opened and a pair of round brown eyes appeared.

'Yes?' said the owner of the brown eyes. 'What do you want?'

'Wassup,' said Major. 'I'm looking for Jimmy the Stink.'

The brown eyes which filled the small hole in the doorway looked past Major and fixed upon Minnie.

'Who's that?'

'That's no one,' said Major. 'I'm Major. Tell Jimmy I'm here.'

Without another word, the little hole in the door was shut with a slam.

'What is this place?' said Minnie. 'What do we do now?'

'Now we play a game,' said Major. 'It's called shut the furball up. If you can manage not to say a single word for the next twenty minutes, no matter what happens, I will give you my dinner for tonight. Deal?'

'What's for dinner?'

'Deal or not?'

Minnie thought about it. Last time she'd made a deal with Major, she'd missed out on a breakfast. Then again, she had escaped from the witches with her body intact.

'Deal.'

'Starting now,' said Major.

To which, of course, Minnie was far too smart to respond. Instead she and Major sat in silence for a good twelve minutes as faint noises and voices rumbled and mewled behind the door. Then they heard the noise of locks being unlocked and bolts being unbolted and chains being unchained, and they watched as the sad, heavy, patchy green door creaked open to reveal a very, very old cat in orange robes, his fur as patchy as the paint on the door and his eyes grey and rheumy. He had clearly had grey and white stripes once, but now he just looked salt-and-pepper all over. When he miaowed he had the croakiest voice Minnie had ever heard, and she was desperate to make a joke about sounding like a frog or any number of age-discriminatory remarks, but of course she couldn't.

'Stink,' said Major.

'Mm,' said the old cat. 'They call me Brother Sagacious here. Major, how are you? Come on in. They told me you had a young lady with you. She'll have to stay out here, I'm afraid. This order is strictly toms only, you know that.'

Major looked at Minnie, who in turn looked up and down the narrow alleyway. It was getting dark quickly, and there was no knowing who hung around these parts.

'She comes with me,' said Major. 'She'll behave. Won't you, Minnie?''

Minnie glowered at him more gloweringly than she'd ever glowered before. But she nodded her head and said nothing.

Jimmy the Stink, aka Brother Sagacious, seemed on the verge of saying something, but Minnie looked so frightened and Major looked so determined, he just sighed slowly, stood out of the way, and said, 'Ten minutes. Just ten minutes and then you have to go.'

Meanwhile, back at the edge of the forest, Tuck pressed his paws against the huge structure to feel it rumble even though it terrified him.

'A motorway—it's just a big road,' said Ginger, although she didn't sound convinced.

And that was just a big 'just'. Tuck had seen roads before, mostly from the Burringos' apartment window, but they were much smaller with little cars the size of matchboxes. And of course he'd seen the roads he and Ginger had driven along in the taxi and walked along as far as the forest. But they'd been empty and quiet. This road was a monster in comparison. If it reached a hill, it cut straight through the middle of it; if it reached a dip, it stretched itself down and filled the dip with concrete. And it was full, full, full of traffic. Not just cars—which were scary enough—but big bellowing buses, terrifying tankers and trucks, large lorries, and deafening diesel dumpsters. An endless stream of them, except streams are soft and gentle, and these vehicles rumbled and thundered and boomed and bellowed and blasted their way along the motorway. So an endless white-water river of them perhaps—**anyhoo**, you get the picture. Tuck certainly got the picture. He had stared at them with huge yellow eyes from the top of the pine tree, and even from up there they looked big and scary. Here, at the base of one of the walls that supported the road, they were even worse. You could not only hear them, you could feel them. And when you pressed your paws against the supporting wall . . . eek. He nearly wet himself every time.

'What are we going to do?' he asked Ginger, thinking, 'Don't say cross it, don't say cross it, don't say cross it.'

'We're going to have to cross it,' said Ginger.

'Couldn't we just walk along for a bit to see if we can go under it?'

'We looked from the pine tree, Tuck. We looked as far as we could see in both directions. There aren't even any tunnels, just cuttings and places like this where it sits on the ground. This is our only chance.'

Tuck didn't say anything. What could he say? There was no point in saying he wanted to go home. And he couldn't say he was hungry because they had, of course, eaten the annoying turkey in the tree. And he couldn't say he was cold because it was going to get even colder before it got warmer, as Ginger kept reminding him. So he just hunched down with his legs underneath him; curled his tail tight round himself, making sure he didn't touch the huge supporting wall; and whimpered as quietly as he could. Ginger rolled her eyes and walked a few metres away to look up at the motorway again.

'Gorgonzola,' she said. 'This is going to be fun.'

They stayed like that for hours, Ginger looking at the motorway, Tuck looking at Ginger, the wind growing stronger so that the noise of the traffic swelled and shrank in waves. Here beside the wall the trees had been cleared when the road had been built, and only small bushes and thin saplings popped up from the rocky ground.

Between them lay ancient litter and new leaves, the wind catching them occasionally and whirling them around before letting them settle in a new mess. It was a dead and depressing place, neither man-made nor natural, just the worst of both worlds. As the sky grew dark and the cold of the night became more of a threat than a promise, Ginger suggested they move back into the trees.

'It'll be warmer there,' she said, 'and maybe we'll find some food.'

'Humph,' said Tuck. 'You going to hunt for us, then, are you?'

Ginger looked at him. 'You got a problem, Tuck?'

Tuck said nothing and followed her towards the trees, but halfway there he spotted a movement. Not a potential supper movement either, something bigger than that.

'Ginger,' he said. 'Ginger!'

She turned and he motioned towards the movement, but Ginger ignored him.

'It's nothing,' she said. 'You're just a scaredy-cat.'

'Am not!' said Tuck, who couldn't believe how brave he'd been ever since they'd left the flat.

'You are,' Ginger said. 'You're scared of everything. You're scared of your own shadow, you're scared of every noise and every new thing, and you're going to be too scared to cross that road when we need to.'

'Am not!' said Tuck. 'You're just fat and horrible and lazy, and you can't hunt, and you'd have starved to death by now if it wasn't for me. You couldn't even catch that turkey stuck in the tree!'

'Yeah, whatever. But at least I wasn't scared of it like you were, Tuck. Listen, if you really think there's something over in the trees, go and find out what it is, you chicken.'

Well, that was just about enough for Tuck. He'd had it up to here with Ginger (which isn't very high for you and me, but for a cat it's above their limit). Without another word he pushed Ginger out of the way and ran directly towards where he'd seen something moving in the trees. He dodged a dandelion, pushed past a pile of pine needles, and threw himself straight into the shadows. Ginger was about a third of the way through a mysterious smile when she heard the strangest noise she'd heard since she'd toured with the Chinese opera. It went, '**Aghimiawebb itoooooorcroke**!!'

And then it went quiet. Very, very quiet.

'Tuck?' said Ginger. It was properly dark now, and she could see only about a metre ahead of her. 'Tuck?'

But there was no answer. 'Tuck, please,' she said. 'Don't play games. You're not really a coward. If anything, I'm the one that's scared now.'

And it's true, she was. But being brave isn't about not feeling fear, it's about feeling fear but doing something anyway. So Ginger walked slowly in the direction where she had seen Tuck disappear into the shadows.

'Tuck?' she miaowed softly every so often. 'Tuckerby?'

Suddenly a huge pair of yellow-green eyes appeared beside her. 'You called me Tuckerby!' he said, smiling to reveal his shiny white teeth as well. 'You've never done that before!'

'Agh!' yowled Ginger, every hair on her body standing on its end and her tail bristling like a giant sea sponge. 'Cheeses, you frightened the furballs out of me. I was really worried.'

'Worried? About me?'

'Worried that maybe you needed my help,' said Ginger, licking herself back into shape.

'Well,' said Tuck. 'Maybe. I'm not sure. This thing, what is it? Is it poisonous?'

Ginger followed Tuck's gaze down to his feet and was not all that surprised to find a huge toad lying on his back, pinned to the ground by one of Tuck's front paws. The toad was a very dark green with big brown splodges all over except on his tummy, which was somewhere between white and grey. He was kicking uselessly with his four legs in the air.

'You want let me go?' he hissed at them.

'Are you poisonous?' said Tuck.

'Why you no lick my back and find out, hairball?' said the toad.

Ginger put her nose down and sniffed the toad. He held her eye in a very menacing way.

'Why were you watching us all day?' she said.

'All day!' said Tuck.

'Yeah, he's been sitting under the trees all day watching us. What's the game, Slimey?'

'You want talk, you let me go,' said the toad. 'Maybe I can do something for you. Maybe I get you to other side.'

'You mean where the dead people live?' said Tuck.

'I think he means the other side of the motorway,'

said Ginger. 'Let him go. Let's hear what he has to say.'

'Can't we just eat him?' said Tuck.

Ginger looked at the toad. The toad looked at Tuck. Tuck looked at Ginger. A classic Mexican standoff.

'No,' said Ginger. 'For one thing, we have no garlic, and for another, I want to hear what he has to say.'

His name was Juan Carlos, and like them he was a long way from home. He had grown up in a lagoon on the far side of the country.

'But no future there,' he said. 'Developers buy the land and they reep it up.'

'Oh, that's awful,' said Tuck. 'Can't someone do something?'

'They could but they don't. My family, they have no power. They just sit and glower hour after hour watching mowers devour the flowers. Alone I can do nothing, so I leave. I travel north of the border to the land of opportunity. Big ponds, endless flies. I not to want read about a better life, I want to leev a better life. So I hit road, travel long, long way. All OK until here. I no get across. I wait here two weeks. I watch you, think maybe you find way across. Normally, I no speak to cats—no offence—but I think we help each other, no?'

They were sitting under a rock ledge where Juan Carlos had set up his camp. It was protected from the wind and conveniently close to a large puddle, from which Juan Carlos encouraged them to drink and in which he sat to tell them his story.

'Oh, that's awful,' said Tuck again. He was touched by the story of the road toad far from his abode breaking his code to share his load.

'What do you mean, "help each other"?' said Ginger.

'I watch traffic for two weeks. I see patterns,' said the toad. 'Traffic seems endless but is not. There are breaks in traffic. But you need see them coming. Me, I no see so far. I climb tree, I see break in traffic, but then is too late when I get to road.'

'Aha,' said Ginger. 'I get it.'

'Aha,' said Tuck. 'I don't.'

So Juan Carlos explained it again. 'I watch traffic for two weeks. I see patterns. Traffic seems endless but is not. There are breaks in traffic. But you need see them coming. Me, I no see so far. I climb tree, I see break in traffic, but then is too late when I get to road. You geddeet?'

Tuck nodded and smiled. 'No,' he said. 'Tell me again.'

'I watch TRAFFIC for TWO weeks,' said Juan Carlos. 'You no speak English or sometheeeng?'

'Tuck,' said Ginger. 'J.C. wants us to go up the tree while he waits on the side of the road. We tell him when there's going to be a break in the traffic and then he crosses the road.'

'Oh!' said Tuck. 'I get it! But why doesn't he just come up in the tree himself?'

'Jose Maria Joseph!' said Juan Carlos. '*Este gato es tonto!*'

'Ah, *lo se*,' said Ginger. '*Pero por favor no lo diga.*'

'So,' said Juan Carlos. 'What you think? You help me, I help you?'

'Why should we?' said Ginger. 'Tuck can tell me when I can cross, and then on the other side I'll find a tree from which to signal him.'

'Ginger!' said Tuck. 'But it was Wham Carlos's idea! He's already helped us. Now we have to help in return, or else it won't be fair. Tell him you're joking.'

Ginger rolled her eyes. 'Of course I was joking. I was just in road-toad goad mode.'

And for what seemed like the first time in a long, long while, Ginger let a huge smile crease her face. There was little in life she ever found as amusing as herself.

Jimmy the Sagacious, I mean Brother Stink, oh, you know who I mean, led Major and Minnie to an inner courtyard of the monastery where he now lived. It was called the Temple of Feline Fine, and like the Furom, like much of the world of alley cats, it was well hidden from human eyes. But there the similarities ended. Where the Furom was a musty, towering place with a subtly aggressive energy, the temple, or at least this courtyard of it, was fragrant and calm. Even though it was fully dark by now and the first spots of rain lighted on the breeze, Minnie wanted to lie down and stretch as if she was in the sun. She wanted to hear how on earth Jimmy the etc. had moved from one place to the other, but Major wasted no time in bringing them to the point, and of course there was nothing she could do about it.

'Jimmy,' he said, 'you can probably guess why we're here.'

Jimmy the Stink aka Brother Sagacious gave a little cough and looked Major in the eye. 'I'm guessing I'm looking at a cat who's calling in a debt,' he said.

'I need a favour, Jimmy.'

'Well, I'd be neutered before denying I owe you one, my brother. How can I help?'

So Major told Jimmy about his life with Ginger and how good it had been and then how one day she'd left. About how he'd presumed she was gone for good until an angry witch turned up and kidnapped him. About how he'd read the location spell and smelled Ginger and another cat there and how the—Oh really, do I have to tell you all this? It's not like you might have missed last week's episode or something.

'That's heartbreaking,' said Jimmy when Major had finished. 'I only wish I could guide better energy towards you. But how can I help?'

'I need to get back to the stables and fast. I reckon Ginger's on the way there. If she finds it empty, I don't know how we'll ever find each other again.'

Jimmy looked at Major sagaciously but said nothing.

'I need a car,' said Major. 'A good car and a good driver.'

The old monk opened his grey eyes wide, coughed again, and frowned. 'I see. . . . The thing is, Major, I've been out of the game a long time. I don't have the connections I used to.'

'If it's too much to ask . . .' said Major.

He caught Jimmy's eye, and they looked at each other a while. Each of them with memories of a foreign battle and a sacrifice made in friendship.

'I didn't say that,' said Jimmy slash Sagacious at last.

'TIME'S UP!' said Minnie. 'Look! Twenty whole minutes, I did it, I did it. Woo-hoo! Double dinner and victory smugness! Now, where's my plates of nosh? Sagacious? Sagacious! I bet you've been sagging for ages, look at ya, **ah ah ah ah ah**.'

Without a word between them, Major and Jimmy the Stink (definitely not Brother Sagacious right at that moment) pinned Minnie to the ground, each with a paw over her mouth. Jimmy looked at his old friend across the writhing ball of fluff beneath them.

'Major, I will do everything in my power to reunite you with Ginger. But it will be dangerous. Just don't say I didn't warn you.'

A BIT OF A MESS ON THE MOTORWAY

Juan Carlos sat on the side of the motorway. *Zoom! Zzzoooom! Brrr . . . brrrr . . . BRR . . . ZOOM!* went the cars and lorries and buses and vans and trucks and motorbikes as they passed him. Have you ever been near a motorway without being in a car? I wouldn't if I were you. It's different from a normal road. The cars are travelling twice as fast, for one thing, and they're not looking out for lights or corners or pedestrians or toads or anything at all. A motorway is a very frightening place to be if you're not in a car. If you don't believe me, wind down the windows next time you're driving along one. Exactly. And that's how it feels for you and me.

Imagine how much worse it would be if you were wet and slimy and the size of a toad. Poor Juan Carlos. But he stuck it out because he was a determined amphibian. He blinked the raindrops out of his eyes and stared not at the traffic, not at the roadkill which had croaked it making earlier attempts at crossing the road, but at a large pine tree at the edge of the forest. *ZooommmmmMMM! wwwwwWWWWOOOWwungggg* went the traffic behind him. Still no movement from the tree. Juan Carlos didn't let himself wonder if the cats had done a runner on him, and of course he didn't succumb to the temptation to hop across the road until he got his signal. No. He just sat and waited.

Meanwhile up in the tree Ginger and Tuck were—surprise, surprise—having a fight.

'I'm not going out there,' said Tuck. 'You go!'

'I have to stay here and watch for the gap in the traffic,' said Ginger.

'Why can't I stay here and watch for the gap in the traffic.'

'Because you're too st-st-strangely heavier than I am.'

'I'm not. You're fat and I'm fin, fine, and fit.'

'Exactly,' said Ginger. 'You're full of muscle.'

'Exactly.'

'And as everyone knows, muscle is one-third heavier than fat.'

Tuck didn't have an answer for that.

'How about a compromise?' said Ginger. 'You go out to the end of the branch, and when I give the signal you jump up and down on it. If it doesn't work, then I'll go out and try again, and if you're right, well, you can call me fatso for the rest of the journey.'

Tuck thought about this for a while, but then he remembered he'd already been thinking about something a minute before and too much thinking made his head hurt.

'Oh, go on then,' he said. 'But I'm doing this for the toad, not for you.'

And so Tuck left the relatively dry shelter of the greenery near the trunk and walked out onto the branch which Juan Carlos and Ginger had agreed would make the best signalling point. It felt like a long way out. It felt like he was walking the gangplank in a not-very-true-to-life pirate movie. When he and Ginger had been climbing the first tree, they'd stuck close to the trunk all the way up. This tree wasn't quite that high, but out here, towards the end of a branch, things were a lot wobblier.

'**Oo-ooh**,' said Tuck. 'Ee-ee.'

'You need to get further out,' Ginger yelled from behind him. 'You need to be able to bounce the branch. Unless you're too scared?'

Well, as we know, Tuck didn't like being told he was scared of anything (even though he was scared of everything, especially vacuum cleaners), so he pushed himself on.

'Aa-aah,' he said. Then 'Uu-uu' as the branch got wobblier still. It was wetter out here, and the wood beneath his feet was slippery. The ground seemed a very long way down.

'Further,' he heard Ginger shout. 'All the way!'

And then Tuck slipped. He felt it happening but could do nothing about it. His two right feet fell to the right of the branch, and his two left feet fell to the left of it. He landed heavily on his stomach, and the whole branch bounced beneath his weight, the ground coming slightly closer and then going slightly further away again.

'That'll do,' said Ginger. 'Now just wait there.'

Tuck was too scared to tell Ginger what he thought of her just then. He pulled his feet back onto the branch and sat crouching there, mewling quietly. After a while he summoned up the courage to turn around. He could see Ginger staring from her safe, dry, and relatively comfortable vantage point down at the road.

'Hurry up!' he said. 'I don't like it here.'

Ginger ignored him at first, but then she seemed to see something further up the motorway in the direction from which all the traffic was coming.

'What's the capital of France?' she said.

'What?'

'I was just wondering if anyone knew what the capital of France was?'

'I know!' said Tuck.

'You see, I really want to know, but I just don't know what it could be.'

'I know!' said Tuck sitting up tall with one paw in the air.

'Spit and polish,' said Ginger, 'if only there was someone who knew. Does anyone know what the capital of France is?'

'Me! Me!' said Tuck, jumping up and down as high as he could with his paw in the air.

'Shame,' said Ginger.

'Me, me, me!' yelled Tuck, waving both his front paws above his head and jumping, jumping, jumping to get her attention. 'I know, pick me! Whoa!'

Well, are you wondering why he 'Whoa'd' when he wanted to wow Ginger with his worldly wisdom? Nah, you've guessed it, I know you have. All that jumping up and down had made the branch underneath him bend to the very limits of its flexibility. Tuck was so excited to answer the question he didn't notice this as it bent down, but when it bounced up again he had to hang on with all ten claws to stop being thrown off.

'**Wooo**,' he said. 'Don't like it.'

Down beside the motorway Juan Carlos did like it. He'd been staring at the branch and had seen it wobble when Tuck slipped, but he didn't think that could be the signal. Now he saw it flailing around massively like it was blowing in a storm. '*Vamos*!' he yelled out to himself. '*Vamonos*!' and as soon as he saw a gap in the traffic, out he hopped. Hop hop. Hoppedy hop. Hop hop hop. He'd estimated he'd make it across the motorway in two or three jumps, but it was far wider than he thought. Eight hops, nine hops, this was getting tiring and he wasn't even halfway across. Suddenly lights appeared around the bend in the road. The next stream of traffic was arriving. Juan Carlos said a very, very, very bad word in Spanish and hopped like his life depended on it. Like? There was no 'like'. His life did depend on it. Hoppedy hoppedy hophophophophophophophop . . . aghh! Did he make it? Or did the lights come upon him faster than he expected and splatter him flat and slimy across the tarmac?

'Did he make it?' yelled Ginger.

'Feel sick,' said Tuck, coming back off the branch to the safety of the trunk.

'Oh no,' said Ginger. 'Why do you feel sick? Did you see him get flattened?'

'No, wobbly branch sick. Seasick sick,' said Tuck. 'Toxic Tuck sick. Eugh, blurgh, eegh.'

'What about Juan Carlos, though. Did he make it?'

Tuck suddenly understood what Ginger was saying. Without another word he ran back out to the end of the branch, even further than he'd gone before, so far that it bent under his weight without him even jumping. He squinted and peered and gazed and stared out at the motorway. There was an awful looking stain in the middle of the far lane, but beyond that, on top of the crash barrier on the far side of the road, he saw a very happy toad jumping up and down and waving with both his little front arms. Tuck waved back and then remembered he was scared of being so far out on the branch and ran back to the trunk.

'He made it,' Tuck said to Ginger. 'He seemed to be mouthing something about a grassy ass. Do you think there's a donkey over there or something?'

'Oh, thank heavens,' said Ginger, and in a rare and unexpected show of emotion she actually put her arms around Tuck. 'Oh, how wonderful. I was so worried, I couldn't have lived with myself.'

'It's F by the way' said Tuck.

'What?'

'F.'

'What's F?'

'The capital of France. Did I get it right?'

Ginger took her arms back from Tuck so that he could see her roll her eyes. Then she said to him, 'Come on, Einstein, it's your turn. Down you go and wait for the signal.'

'Gulp,' said Tuck.

Well, crossing the road when you're a desperate toad keen to build a life on the other side in clean ponds, good health care and a land of opportunity is one thing. Doing it when you're a scaredy-cat is quite another. It took

Tuck ten tentative tries to even get close to the road.

wwwwwwww WWWOOOWwung

wwwwwwww WWWOOOWwungggg

wwwww WWWOOOWwungggg

It was far louder than anything Tuck had ever heard before, far louder and faster and scarier and deadlier. He looked up at the tree and saw Ginger standing at the junction of the branches. She had hooked her front paws under her armpits and was waving her elbows up and down, pushing her head back and forwards at the same time.

'I'm not a chicken!' shouted Tuck up to her, but of course she was far too far away to hear him. She just strutted out along the branch, head back and forth, elbows flapping, pausing now and then to peck something from the wood beneath her feet.

Well, if Tuck couldn't tell her, he was just going to have to show her. Humph. So he walked straight up the very side of the road, jumped up onto the crash barrier, tail in the air like he just didn't care, and ignored the humbling thundering rumbling of a passing juggernaut.

Ginger looked down and saw him and ran straight back towards the main shaft of the tree. She stood there for at least half an hour staring upstream to look for a gap in the traffic. It was dark by now, the temperature down, and the stars starting to pop out. Tuck thought if Ginger didn't hurry up, they might be stuck there for another night. Or worse, they'd be stuck on different sides of the motorway for a night. His anger at her paltry poultry puss-take began to fade and his fear of the monstrous, great vehicles behind him began to return. Then he saw

Ginger suddenly run out to the end of the branch. She ran so far to the very, very end that it bent right down to the branch below it. That was the signal.

Tuck turned toward the motorway and tried to take his first step forward. But he found his feet wouldn't move. He knew in his head he had to cross the road, he knew in his heart he trusted Ginger, but in his feet he seemed only to know to stay where he was. He looked up helplessly at Ginger who was bouncing so far up and down on the branch she looked like a bungee jumper who'd overestimated the amount of elastic she needed. He knew he should go.

'Come on, Tuck,' he said. 'Brave Tuck. Not chicken Tuck. Brave.'

The last car zoomed past, and the tarmac stretched out empty before him like a huge stage waiting for his performance. Tuck moved one foot slightly forward. Ginger was shouting something; in the lack of traffic he could almost hear it, and he guessed it would be something rude. It sounded like 'to rate' or 'to Kate' or something he wouldn't understand. So he forced himself on, forced one foot in front of the other until before he knew it he was walking. Walking across the road.

'Two mates!' he could hear Ginger screaming behind him. 'To date!' Well, that didn't make sense, but Tuck pushed himself on so he couldn't hear it.

Then he heard a noise, and he looked to his right and saw, not a hundred metres away, three lanes of traffic coming around the bend. He'd left it too late. That's what Ginger had been shouting: 'Too late! TOO

LATE!!' And now here he was, slap bang in the middle of the motorway with a van in the left lane, a lorry in the middle lane, and a bus in the right lane—all bearing down on him at speed.

No matter what Tuck did now, there was no way he could get to the other side. And it was too late to go back to where he'd come from. He stared at the front of the bus, the fastest of the three vehicles, and watched it grow bigger and bigger and bigger in his vision. But still his feet didn't move.

A BIT OF A DOG 2

Bumton was not a part of town you'd want to visit at night. In fact, Bumton wasn't a part of town you'd want to visit during the day. In fact, Bumton wasn't a part of town. It was the name of a dry cleaner's in Crapton, a seedy part of town to the south of the city where the action now takes us. Crapton was riddled with really rough riff-raff, tough guys who'd attack with a clacky back-smack as soon as look at you. If you stopped your car at every red light in Crapton, you'd never get anywhere. That was if you had a car without the local hoodlums stripping it and selling the parts. Bumton of Crapton's was not the only building in that part of town covered with graffiti—they all were. And most of their windows were broken, and the streets were covered in litter. It was well known that any cat that crept into cruddy Crapton could easily come a cropper, getting crimped and cropped and carried crying to the Crapton crypt. But it was to Crapton that Brother Sagacious sent Major and Minnie to find a car.

'**Lummocks**,' said Minnie. 'What a dump! We're more likely to leave here in a coat than in a car. You sure this is the right place?'

Major ignored her. He'd discovered that if he ever answered Minnie's first question, she only came back with a second or a third. And if he told her to shut up, she'd talk more and more. He sniffed the air, looked up and down the desolate street where they found themselves, and walked on.

'How much further is it?' said Minnie.

'Not far,' Major said before he could stop himself.

'Not far? Not far? 'Ow far's that? Too far for fair fur, that's for sure. What time is it? Can I 'elp? What's the street called?'

Major did a big gingery sigh and padded on.

'It's next left,' he said. 'That alley over there.'

They stopped and looked across the road to the alley. It didn't look very inviting. An old pram lay across the entrance, spilling tins and plastic bags onto the pavement. Beside it stood a large rubbish bin with its lid missing.

'Ooh, you do take me to some lovely places,' said Minnie.

The alley itself was dark. On one side the huge great wall of a warehouse blocked out the sun. On the other ran a tall, black fence interspersed with locked gates. It smelled of rotting rubbish and rat poo. Major had grown up on the streets, and this kind of environment didn't disturb him with anything but memories, but as he and Minnie walked down the dim, dank, damp dump of an alleyway, he noticed she had gone very quiet beside him.

'Don't worry, dude,' he said. 'We can trust Jimmy the S.'

But Major didn't sound as certain of that as he'd intended to. Towards the end of the alley, in the one spot where a bit of sunlight reflected off the high warehouse windows and lit the tarmac from a dull black to a dull grey, they found the last gate in the fence. It wasn't locked. Major pushed at it cautiously with his nose, and it swung open with a creepy creak.

'You looking for me?' said a husky French voice behind them.

Both cats spun round and found themselves facing a large poodle. Her hair was shaved in fancy ways on her body, legs, and tail so that she looked like she was wearing a series of cream pompoms.

'Doubt it!' said Minnie, giving the poodle a slow look up and down. 'Buzz off, doggy.'

'We're looking for Sid,' said Major.

'*Oui*, Cyd, *c'est moi*,' said the poodle. 'I understand you boys are looking for ze lift, *oui*?'

'Oh. We were expecting a— I mean . . . a—'

'A cat. Or a male dog?' said the poodle. 'But instead you got me. Life's like that, *n'est-ce pas*?'

'*Oui*,' said Major. 'Indeed.'

'What's with the wee?' said Minnie. 'You want to go again already?'

Major looked at Cyd and Cyd looked at Minnie. Then Cyd asked if the floor rag was coming with them.

Her car was parked two streets away. She'd meet zem in ze alley for safety's sake, she said. There were people out looking for her, and she couldn't afford to take risks. Minnie asked her what people and why they were looking, but the poodle ignored her and said 'Come zis way.' The car was a Purrgeot, an old-fashioned model with a huge boot and worn-out seating. It had a very distinctive smell, a mixture of old leather, perfume, and French paperbacks. That and the unmistakeable smell of dog. The poodle told them to get in while she went to the front and cranked up the engine.

'**Pwoar**!' said Minnie as she climbed into the back. 'Whassat awful smell?'

'Minnie,' hissed Major. 'Don't be so rude. This poodle is on the run too, and she's probably taking risks to help us.'

'Don't peg that piggy pong on the pug,' said Minnie. 'I reckon you let one rip!'

But before Major could respond to this, they both felt the car jerk to life. Cyd appeared at the side window with the crank in her mouth. She dropped it through the open back window so that it just missed Minnie's tail.

'Oh,' Cyd said. 'So sorry.'

Then she climbed into the driver's seat, fiddled with the controls, put a chew toy in her mouth, and they were off. Now, as you know, not all dogs smell bad to us humans. But cats generally can't stand the smell of dogs, not unless they're washed three times a week with lavender shampoo and then sprayed with fancy perfume. Needless to say, whatever Cyd's history, she no longer had such a lifestyle. She was a pursued poodle in a pre-loved Purrgeot. You and I might have thought she was a bit fusty, but for Major it was so bad he had to open his window very subtly and sit with his nose close to the airstream. As for Minnie, she was a mucky moggie and didn't give a fig for the froggy dog's foggy fug, but she wasn't going to let the poodle get away with nearly dropping a crank on her tail.

''Ere, Frenchy,' she said. 'Where d'you get your hair done, eh?'

'Don't worry, darling,' said the poodle over her shoulder. 'You couldn't afford it.'

Major smirked and looked out the window. This was going to be an interesting ride.

They took backstreets all the way out of town, a long and circuitous route that avoided the city centre and all the streets where a police station might be. The car rumbled and grumbled, but it didn't let them down.

'Where you from?' said Major when they'd been driving for an hour or so.

'I was born in Marseille,' said Cyd, 'but I grew up in Malta. You know it? It is in the Mediterranean sea.'

'A little,' said Major. He'd been there with Ginger in the early days, when they were so in love it felt like the world belonged to them. He didn't want to talk about it.

'I've heard Malta's quite grubby,' said Minnie.

'Probably the part you would most likely visit,' sniffed the poodle. 'I've never seen that side of it.'

'Ladies,' said Major. 'Enough. You, Cyd, you're bigger than this. And, Minnie, don't meddle with a madame from the middle of the Med. You'll only get in a maddening muddle.'

Somehow Minnie resisted responding to this, and the three animals sat in silence for a while. Major kept his nose close to the window and watched the sky darken. If he had worked things out correctly, he might be about to see Ginger again, and that gave him plenty to think about. Cyd gnawed on her chew toy in silence, punctuating its squeaks only with pulls on a hip flask she kept beside the handbrake. And Minnie fell fast asleep on the back seat, dreaming dreams of dynamite and deadly derring-dos.

Major must have slept too because when he next opened his eyes they were on the motorway already. It was dark, and he could see only as far as the headlights would allow. To the left of the car was the great dark forestiness of the Great Dark Forest; to the right, three lanes of traffic coming the other way down the busy road. Beyond that, more forest.

'Where are we?' he asked Cyd.

The poodle shrugged her shoulders. 'No idea. We 'ave been on ze autoroute for maybe 'alf an hour.'

Major looked out at the blackness and wondered if Ginger had taken this same route in recent months. Or—and he shuddered at the thought—if she'd maybe decided to cross the forest on paw. Which meant of course crossing the motorway too.

Then Cyd shouted, '**Zut alors**!,' and started braking hard. Minnie slid forward off the back seat and landed with a painful bump on the floor, and Major turned to see that a white panel van had crossed the central reservation and driven directly into the road in front of them. Cyd was slowing them so quickly that the tyres of the old Purrgeot filled their senses: they could smell burning rubber, they could see smoke trailing behind them, they could feel the car wobbling and wibbling as it lost traction, they could hear the tyres screaming on the tarmac beneath them, and they could taste the acrid taste of fear because no way would they slow down enough to avoid hitting the white panel van.

A BIT OF BLOODTHIRSTY REVENGE

Now, I know what you're thinking. You're thinking, 'Golly jeepers, isn't this a great book. I'm going to recommend it to all my friends, and I can't wait to see the movie.' And you're thinking, 'Gosh, cats/motorway/ coincidence?' And you're thinking most of all, 'Thank goodness there's no more nonsense about those awful witches.' Well, two out of three ain't bad. Because give me a *B*, give me a *U*, give me an *RR*, *Ingo*! (Try that again with arm gestures. It works really well.)

When we last left Rodney Burringo, he was steaming and wilted and had just blown up a little old lady. Well, we all know what that feels like, but let me tell you, his day didn't get any better when Janice came stumbling downstairs to complain about the noise and then started screaming when she saw the state of her front door.

'Shut up, you stupid witch!' shouted Rodney, which of course didn't help either of their moods.

'My door!' howled Janice. 'What have you done to my blooming door?!'

And then she saw that the sprinkler system had been set off and poured water all over her living room.

'My soft furnishings!' she screamed. 'My carpet and,

boo hoo hoo, my television!' Then she stopped screaming and turned with a horrifyingly evil look at Rodney.

'What have you done?' she hissed at him. 'What did you do?'

'It wasn't me,' Rodney snapped back at her. 'It was those cats! That stupid fluffy mongrel you brought back from the cat shelter and that ginger lump. They blew up the door and escaped.'

Well, it's a good job you're hearing this third-hand because if you'd been there you would have witnessed the most horrible metamorphosis since the Incredible Hulk. Janice scowled so hard that her ears shot into points which pierced the brim of her hat. Her nose hooked over so far that it scratched the warts on the end of her chin. Her breath grew rank and toxic, her teeth turned pointy and yellow. Her nails extended into curling grey claws, and her spine stuck out from the skin of her back.

'**Raaaaaaa**!' she screamed. 'Raaaaa! I'm going to get them and squeeze them so hard that their guts come out of their bumholes! I'm going to wear their eyeballs like a pearl necklace, and I'm going to make loofahs from their tails! Get me them, get me them, get me them **NOWWWWWW**!'

'Phwoar,' said Rodney, who was not unaffected by the sight before him. 'Don't you worry, your royal hotness. I won't rest until all four of them are back in this house. I'll not quit until you have whatever you want. You deserve no less. I am a slave to your utter witchiness. I'll start on it straightaway! Now give me a hand, and help me scrape this little old lady off the corridor walls before anyone sees.'

And so they scraped and sponged and tidied. Then, while Janice called the door replacement company, Rodney started planning.

The next night the Burringos' shiny new apartment door was opened to twenty-two visitors. To anyone who saw these visitors crossing the building's lobby or riding up in the lift they looked like normal people (except of course there's no such thing). But once that shiny new door was closed behind them, they shed their disguises and revealed themselves for the abysmal, atrocious, awful animals they were. For they were witches, every last one of them. Tall and short, fat and thin, young and old, all quite extreme, in fact. Not a single mid-height, mid-weight, middle-aged one amongst them. Rodney and Janice felt quite mundane by comparison, but they did not dwell on such trivialities. For Rodney had invoked the rules of his coven and called them all together to 'protect the honour of a fellow witch against mischievous felines' (1753 Witching Act, claws 28b).

Together the twenty-four witches spoke hideous spells in calm and calculated tones and plotted the most evil of plans, that is, they drew up a roster so that every night every part of the city would be observed by them. Not only that, they mapped out the route between the Burringos' apartment and the stables where Rodney had found Major. They couldn't fly during the day of course, but as soon as any of the cats appeared in the open at night-time, the alarm would be raised. Then the fury of the Burringos would be unleashed, and the poor posse of pussies would be pests put in the past. Mwah ha. Mwah

ha ha. Mwah ha ha ha ha ha ha!!!

Let's just hope the cats don't step outside at night, eh?

Now, you're probably wondering what happened to Tuck. I'm not going to drag this out. I'm not going to divert you with fascinating stories of how huge mountain ranges are constantly forming under the sea and that's what causes earthquakes. Nor point out that bananas, like oranges, are formed in segments—every banana having exactly three. Don't believe me? Open a banana, take a bite, then stick your finger into the end of it and see what happens. Fascinating! But irrelevant, I know, so no more of that stuff. Oh coconuts no. This is what happened to Tuck:

So, you've got a six-lane motorway (three lanes in each direction) with an irregular gap in the traffic. You've got a new cluster of traffic approaching from a north-easterly direction with, at the front, three large vehicles. These are: a van in the left-hand lane carrying a family of Italian musicians on their way home from a wedding, a tanker lorry in the middle lane with a full load of liquid on its way to deliver to restaurants across the city, a bus in the right-hand lane carrying a party of animal rights activists on their way home from a weekend retreat. And in the blue corner you've got a rather fit but essentially less-than-superbly-intelligent black cat who is frozen in the headlights. The average speed of the three above-mentioned vehicles is 112 kilometres per hour. The cat is not moving.

The bus, the fastest of the three vehicles, was being driven by a man by the name of Dick Pilchard. He was seventy-five and had been driving buses for fifty-five years. He no longer enjoyed his job and found one of the few things that gave it any interest was flattening as many animals as possible into the road. It was possibly for this reason that as his bus came round the bend in the road he started accelerating despite already being above the speed limit. The passengers in the front seat behind and slightly above Dick Pilchard were an animal-loving mother and son by the name of Juliet and Billie Balcony. Billy was twenty-eight years old and still lived at home. Nuff said. It was Juliet Balcony, a middle-aged woman with surprisingly long vision, who first saw Tuck.

The tanker lorry, the slowest of the vehicles, was driven by a rather large woman by the name of Florence Airport, more commonly known by her nickname of Heavy Flo. Flo was (and indeed still is) a contract driver for Peter Parsons Pickles and Sauces and had recently consumed five cups of coffee from the Speedy Coffee Shop and Service Centre. She was admiring her newest tattoo as she came around the bend and didn't see Tuck at all.

The Italian musicians in the white van, the Aisingacreppis, were a family of four men, three women, two boys and four girls, all on the podgy side of normal. You might have heard one of their later songs, '*C'è un gatto nero sul autostrada*'. The father of the family, Beppe Giuseppe Aisingacreppi, a round-faced and cheerful man, was driving the van. He saw Tuck at the same time as he saw the bus full of animal rights' activists, two lanes to his right, veer in front of the tanker lorry between them and then in front of him and his family.

At the inquest which followed the crash it became clear that this happened because Juliet Balcony had seen Dick Pilchard speeding towards Tuck and— as a committed advocate of the rights of animals to a happy and healthy life—had thrown herself onto the steering wheel 'to save the poor mite's little life'. Beppe Giuseppe was driving too fast and with too heavy a load (it being pasta season) to brake in time to avoid hitting the bus. Accordingly, he swerved to the right so that all the Aisingacreppis sang-slash-screamed as one (it was never easy to tell the difference with them) as they in turn veered across the trajectory of the tanker lorry. The bus full of animal lovers and the van full of pasta lovers swerved and swam, swung and swang and switched lanes and swapped places on the motorway just before they reached Tuck.

And what did Tuck do? Well, he just sat there, still frozen with his yellow eyes wide open and watched them cross lanes in front of him and then zoom past on either side. Which left just Flo's tanker lorry in the middle lane bearing down on him.

Let's look what happened to the bus. Well, it didn't stay in its new position in the left-hand lane. Oh no. As Dick Pilchard fought off Juliet Balcony, it swerved and swayed and wibbled and wobbled until at last, when Dick somewhat belatedly applied the brakes, it screeched to a halt, turned a ninety-degree angle and rolled onto its side. Ouch! Naturally, all those with their seat belts done up were unharmed, but everyone else had to wear one of those hideous white collar things for months.

Things weren't much less hairy for the occupants of the van. As you might have worked out by now, they didn't stop veering across the motorway when they reached the inside lane where the bus had previously been. Despite Beppe Giuseppe Aisingacreppi's best efforts, they smashed through the crash barrier on that side of the road and into the path of the three lanes of traffic coming up from the city. And what was the first vehicle they encountered there? **Yugoddit**. It was a throbbing old Purrgeot containing you-know-who.

And what of Heavy Flo and her tanker? Did she squash Tuck as flat as a bat whacked with a mat? Well, Flo might have been a bit zippy on the coffee, and she might have been a little late in getting her eyes off her still-glistening ink, but Flo was a pro, don't you know. Later media reports of her as 'The Girl with the Saggin' Tattoo' were unkind. For Flo took an immediate assessment of the situation as first the bus full of activists and then the van full of Italians veered across her path, and she did what you or I would do in the same situation. She screamed her head off with the worst swear word she could think of and jammed both feet on the brake.

Have you ever seen a full tanker go from 110 **kayemperaitch** to zero in five seconds? It ain't pretty. Unless, of course, said tanker is about to run over you and kill you. So Tuck watched with wider and wider eyes as the grille of Flo's tanker got closer and closer to him until, as if by magic, it was suddenly spun around him as the lorry jack-knifed into the slow lane and then around Tuck into the middle lane, and then on again into the fast lane and, still not stopping, into the nearest lane of traffic coming up from the city. Now, the Aisingacreppis' van had just come to a stop in this lane, and at that very moment Beppe Giuseppe and his brother, preppy Pepe, were crossing themselves and crying and watching a heavy old Purrgeot zooming straight up towards them, a cursing poodle and strangely Zen-like ginger cat framed in its windscreen.

'Is the end,' said Beppe. 'We all gonna die!'

But just then the back end of Flo's tanker came swinging around and shoved the Aisingacreppis' van out of the way and into the far lane, where there were no other cars at all. Still the tanker carried on swinging so that its arc moved out of the way of the braking Purrgeot just in time for them to miss one another. Good job! For by now the French car was being driven by a dog with one front paw over her eyes and the other unscrewing her hip flask.

On and on Flo's tanker swung until it ended up facing the way it had started. Then, as its hydraulic brakes exploded in loud bangs and its tyres did the same, the tanker shuddered, fell over, and split along its entire side. The tasty sauce it had been due to deliver to the finest eateries of the city poured out and started spreading back up the motorway. Can you imagine the carnage? Not to mention the busnage, lorrynage, and vannage? Imagine the noises of screeching brakes, exploding tyres, screaming drivers, splitting metal, slopping brown sauce. But in the middle of this sat, very still and wide-eyed, a familiar black cat.

'**Oooh**,' said Tuck. 'That was lucky. I thought I'd stopped too soon.'

Then he smelled something. Can you guess what it was? It was not the stinky stench of hydraulic liquid boiled to gas. Nor the acrid acidity of animal activists' recently soiled underwear. Nor was it the burning of old Purrgeot brake discs. No, no, no. It was the smell of a wave of mushroom sauce coming out of Flo's torn and twisted tanker.

'Ginger!' Tuck yelled at the top of his voice. 'Ginger, look! We're at the mushroom-sauce seaside, and the tide's coming in!' And without a second thought (because let's face it, the first one wasn't particularly great) he ran to the tasty taupe for which he'd always hoped. Once there he lapped and lapped and lapped whilst the sauce grew knee deep around him (asterisk re cats' knees, but not now, OK?).

Can you imagine a scene more conducive to purring? First of all, there's Tuck purring so hard he was gargling half the sauce he swallowed back up again. Then there was Ginger, who had of course watched the entire scene in horror from the pine tree. She came running down and met Tuck in the lake of mushroom sauce, so relieved to see him still alive that she forgot herself and sniffed his bum. The old Purrgeot on the other side of the road was now empty, and its occupants had come over to see what all the fuss was about. As Major crossed the central reservation he first saw a large, athletic black cat who seemed to have taken it upon himself to clear up the spilt goods from the tarmac. Beside this cat was a redhead who looked a lot like . . . Oh my cod.

'Ginger,' said Major. But his voice was so full of emotion he could barely speak her name. 'Ginger.'

Ginger looked up, not at the sound of her name but at something her sixth sense told her was of vital importance. She squinted into the distance to see humans getting out of vehicles, inspecting broken violins, 'It's Just Not Fur' placards and smudgy biceps. But then she looked closer and a little to the right, and she saw a cat that looked like . . . O.M.C. Well, I admit it. There was not much purring as she and Major approached each other with undeniable tears on their faces.

'Major,' said Ginger.

'Ginger,' said Major.

'I didn't leave you,' she said.

'I know,' said Major. 'I came to get you. I was in that apartment. I escaped and that's why I'm here.'

And they broke down in a caterwaul which both of them would later deny ever happened. All they could think was that all the trials and tribulations and travelling and trauma had been worth it for this one moment. They were together again and need never part. They held each other in a tight embrace, unable to speak beyond a muted purr that said more than words ever could.

''Ere!' said Minnie, who'd walked up beside them. ''Oo's he then?'

Ginger looked up to see her pointing over at Tuck, his muscly silhouette set off by the hazy rage of beige around him.

'That's Tuck,' said Major.

'That's right,' said Ginger, amazed. 'How did you know? That's Tuck.'

'Phwoar,' said Minnie. ''E's a bit of all right, inny! Somebody better pass me a hot tin roof!'

And then it happened.

What do you mean, 'What happened?' Are you choking or something? *It* happened. Oh, come on. You're making me feel like Juan Carlos must have felt when Tuck didn't get it about the signal from the tree. Come on, folks: Where is this scene taking place? What time of day is it? Who has got a roster watching over anything unusual happening between the city and Major's stables?

Oh no?

Oh yes.

THE BIT AFTER THAT BIT ON THE MOTORWAY

Tra la la la la la. I'm going to talk about lots of irrelevant stuff from a completely different part of the plot so that you're kept in a greater state of suspension than bungee jumping in stockings in Alaska ('great state', get it? As in 'Alaska's a state which is really big', which is another word for 'great'? Yes? No? Oh, why do I bother?). Let's look at what happened to Juan Carlos next. Or what about Cyd—would you like to hear how she ended up with a post-traumatic stress counsellor as an owner? I'm sure you'd love to hear all about the legal wrangling that took place during the inquest that followed the crash. And about Heavy Flo's tattoo, which needed complete redrawing after such a severe smudging. Or what about the Aisingacreppis and their international one-hit wonder, the only-ever Italian-language song to get to number one in Italy? There are so many places I could take this plot now, but you know what? Inquest, ink mess, sing quest, **BYAH**! Let's get back to the action. (Asterisk: cats do have knees.)

The witch on patrol over the motorway at the time of the pile-up was Claire Blair. Yes, that Claire Blair, the founder of Claire Blair's Fair Hair Care, the shampoo that makes blondes look even blonder. Didn't you know that was a magic potion? Well, you do now. Claire Blair stole the recipe from a stern old hairdresser in the twenties known as Severe Bob and then, as we all know, made millions from a savvy use of marketing and distribution rights. Now, making a lot of money is a funny old thing (and must never, *never,* NEVER! be confused with 'success', remember that).

You see, whilst many people would like to make a lot of money themselves, they often hate to see other people doing it. I say 'many people', but I should also say 'all witches'. Witches are the most money-grabbing, avaricious, gold-digging, materialistic meanies you've ever heard of. They *always* confuse making a lot of money with success no matter how miserable they become in the process. Well, you can imagine how popular Claire Blair was with all the other witches! That's right—not very. In fact, they hated her guts and were forever complaining that Claire should share her Fair Hair Care ware. They called her a 'sell-out', which is a word that means 'You made more money than I did'. And of course it didn't help that Claire was absolutely beautiful and had the most perfect body of any witch on earth. Can you imagine the green that the other witches turned with their foul and smelly envy? Poor Claire, if she wasn't such a witch, you'd feel sorry for her. All the money in the world, the perfect figure, a cute little nose, and nobody loved her.

If that happened to you or me, we'd realise we needed to change friends, but Claire had a poorly developed sense of self and so was always trying to impress the other witches in the hope that their admiration would make her life complete. Sad, isn't it? Even if not entirely relevant. **Bendyways**, there Claire was, cruising at a height of I-don't-know-how-many metres above the high/free/motorway, looking at the strip of red lights moving away from the city and the strip of white lights moving towards it, when suddenly there was the most enormous **crash, bang, slop-slop** below her.

'Goodness,' thought Claire. 'I wonder what that was?'

And she swooped down for a look, the wind blowing her beautiful hair out behind her. The smell of mushroom sauce was just tickling her petite and perfectly formed nose when what did she spot in the middle of all the spilled sauce and carnage? That's right. Not one, not two, not three, but all four cats hugging and weeping and phwoaring and lapping in the middle of the road.

'Oh my!' said Claire to herself. 'Oh me, oh my, oh ma, I'm going to be a star!'

And without a further thought she took out her extremely expensive finely-crafted-from-Norwegian-wood wand and pointed it at the cats. But Claire had acted too soon. Like many of us, she had forgotten to think in the heat of the moment. She had completely forgotten that her wand was still in Create Shampoo mode.

'Eugh!' said Tuck down on the ground. 'This mushroom sauce suddenly tastes really soapy.'

And he spat his last mouthful of liquid out and tried licking the soapy taste of it off his tongue. Then he blinked and blinked again because he couldn't believe his eyes. All the mushroom sauce around him had turned to soapy suds of shampoo.

'Ginger!' he yelled soapily. 'Where's my sauce gone?'

Ginger and Major and Minnie all looked over at him strangely, and then their eyes grew wide as they too saw the sauce turning to suds. ''Ere, that's a bit weird, innit?' said Minnie. 'It's like a magic spell or something.'

'A magic spell?!' said Ginger.

'Run!' said Major, and then, as Ginger joined in, 'Run, run, run!'

But it was too late. For Claire had realised her mistake and changed her wand to the Freeze Cats setting, and within the blink of an eye Tuck and Ginger, Minnie and Major found themselves frozen to the spot. Cyd, who'd watched the whole thing happen from the car, came running over, barking wildly. Juan Carlos, who'd hopped back to see what had happened, started croaking at the top of his voice. But neither of them could attract the attention of the stupid humans, who were more interested in their cars than saving the lives of four fearsome felines. They just thought a barking dog and a croaking frog were a normal part of a multi-vehicle pile-up—and I suppose you can't blame them. I mean, how were they to know otherwise? So it was without any form of human intervention that Claire landed with a dainty swoosh in the middle of the foaming suds and started picking up the frozen cats one by one and shoving them into a catsack-backpack which she'd brought along just in case.

'Stop!' barked Cyd, managing to bite Claire on the bum and ripping a hole in the back of her designer jeans.

'Stop!' croaked Juan Carlos, jumping onto Claire's cloak (toads and frogs—unlike princes and newts—being utterly unafraid of witches).

But Claire didn't care. She simply gave Cyd a ladylike kick and brushed Juan Carlos off with a laugh. Then she jumped back onto her broomstick, the packed catsack-backpack back on her back, and flew straight up into the air before pointing her broomstick towards the city and racing off in a dainty green trail of gas. She left behind a pool of brown shampoo and a very upset dog and toad.

'What is all thees soapy suds?' said Juan Carlos when he realised there was nothing more they could do.

'Sod ze suds,' said Cyd sadly. 'I have a hunch zat bunch are to be munched for a crunchy lunch. Oh, ze poor pussies.'

And with that she shed a little tear, for beneath her cool, hard, French exterior she was a sensitive soul. Juan Carlos cried too, for without the help of the cats he would never have made it over the road to his new life. Then the two of them—but that's a whole other story, and it'll have to wait for a whole other time. Otherwise you'll never get to see our four heroes slaughtered in the most gruesome manner imaginable, and I know how much you're looking forward to that.

Arriving at the Burringos' was one of the happiest moments of Claire Blair's long and actually quite interesting life. She had radioed her news ahead, and by the time she arrived everyone was gathered in the Burringos' living room. Even her sister Cher, who hated

Claire more than anyone there, was waiting in a chair. For it was coven rules: all had to attend to ensure the dishonour of a fellow witch was undone.

'Our heroine returns,' said Rodney as he opened the door to Claire.

'Where are the cats?' said Janice.

'You've got a hole in your jeans,' said Cher.

Claire smiled and said nothing. She just walked into the middle of the living room and pulled the frozen cats out of the catsack-backpack. Well, you can imagine the cackles and applause that greeted each stiff pussy. The witches all started farting horrible green gases until Janice was forced to open a window. Then the coven presented Claire with the Green Claw, a very high honour indeed.

'Well done,' said Rodney. 'And thank you.'

'Er, yes, s'pose,' said Janice, who didn't like the way Rodney looked at Claire.

'It's not fair, she should share,' said Cher, looking at Claire's bare derriere through the tear that needed repair.

Claire didn't care, Cher was always a mare, and it didn't matter how much she stared and glared. All Claire could hear was the applause, and all she could see were the smiles of the other witches around her. Poor Claire. She didn't realise that even this pretence of admiration from the horrible coven of cackling crones would be short-lived and that the next day all the witches would hate her even more than they had before.

'Anyway,' said Janice once the hubbub had died down. 'You must all be awfully tired. You should probably all head home.'

'No!' shouted all the witches. 'Let's party!'

'Na-ah,' said Janice. 'Get lost. We've done all the congratulations, award-presenting, backslapping, coven-dishonour-removal rubbish, and I'm tired. Rodney and I have got a long night of witchery ahead of us tomorrow, and it's almost dawn. Go on, sling your hooked noses.'

I cannot bring myself to describe to you the long, hot, and airless hours the four cats spent in the apartment the next day as they waited for Rodney and Janice to wake up. Well, I can: they were long, hot and airless—what did you expect? Let's skip to later that night, when a yellowy-browny-orangey fog filled the living room, blurring the outlines of the furniture and leaving a fine, rusty dust on all the surfaces. It settled on the copy of *Witch!* magazine that lay open on the dining room table. It settled on the kitchen counter, on the food mixer, shopping bags, and open cans that sat there. And it settled onto the backs of the four thawed-out cats, who sat in two cages in the corner of the room. Major, Minnie, and Ginger in one cage, Tuck in the other.

'**Miaowww**,' yowled Tuck sadly. 'Miaoowww.'

'Chill, dude,' Major mewed across to him. 'If we're going to go, let's go in peace. Meditate with me, man.'

Tuck looked over at Major and at the pretty fluffy cat next to him, whose name he couldn't remember. Then he looked at Ginger, who was nestled in the crook of Major's arm and was licking Major's forehead. She winked at Tuck encouragingly, and this made Tuck sadder still. If Ginger was being nice to him, then things must be in a very sorry state.

'Miaowww,' he said.

Suddenly a crooked figure loomed through the yellow fog between the two cages. It was Janice, looking even more rank and wrinkly than ever.

'What's wrong, my pretty pretty?' she said to Tuck. 'You've got nothing to worry about. In a few minutes you'll be a Purrari!'

For Janice had changed her mind again, sickly fickle cranky-rank and wrinkly witch that she was. Now that she had all the cats together, she'd decided she wanted the very best bits of all four of them in one sublime and streamlined feline. She wanted a black Purrari with soft fluffy fur, fiercely intelligent but with an easy-going personality. The idea had occurred to her the previous night as she'd seen the cats pulled out of the bag one by one. That was why she'd been so impatient to see all the witches leave. She knew it would be a long and complicated spell that would make it possible.

'It says here you need a fire pit,' said Rodney from the dining table. He was bending over the magazine, trying to read the Furmerger Spell through the yellow fog, throwing up red dust as he flicked back and forth between two pages.

'Or a large cooking pot,' snarled Janice, who'd had the rare foresight to read the spell all the way through to the end.

'Oh yeah,' said Rodney, coughing slightly and trying to make out the next instruction.

The spell was of course written in runes, and Rodney's runes were really rusty. Not only that, he'd been cooking since twilight and was already exhausted.

The first half of the spell called for five pairs of pants to be soiled, broiled, and boiled, which of course was toil. It took ages and was causing this strange fog to fill the house. Then Rodney had had to find a teenager with severe acne so he could get together enough fresh pus to squeeze slowly into the boiling pants. After that he'd had to search to the very back of the fridge to find some toe jam and the last of a jar of chocolate bumbits. But find them he had, and now he was ready for the second and far more delicate part of the operation. It was time to prepare the cats.

'"Put pet in pit or pot and pat",' he read, trailing his fingers slowly across the runes as he translated.

'Which one?' said Janice.

'The cooking pot.'

'No, which cat, you moron,' said Janice tetchily. Oh, how she wanted this to work.

Rodney consulted the magazine again and then looked up, wafting the yellow pant-stain fog out of his way. Very slowly he lifted one long index finger. 'That one,' he said, pointing at Tuck.

Poor Tuck. Never the bravest of pussies, he was now at his most terrified. He yowled and cowered and showered Janice with spit as she approached. Well, Janice wasn't about to risk being bitten or scratched, so she went to fetch the one thing she knew could threaten Tuck into submission. She got the vacuum cleaner.

'**Nooo**!' yowled Tuck.

'It can't 'urt you,' said Minnie from the other cage. 'It's just noisy, innit.'

'Dude, it's fine,' said Major

'Tuck, toughen up!' said Ginger.

But poor Tuck was so terrified he simply sat and trembled in the corner of his cage.

'Any more trouble from you,' said Janice, pointing the vacuum cleaner at him, 'and I'll turn this thing on and suck you up into the guts of it. Waa ha ha ha.'

I don't know why she cackled at the end of that sentence, but she did. It was probably the thought of doing something horrible.

'You ready for it?' she said to Rodney. 'Shall I get it out of the cage?'

'It?' said Ginger.

'It?' said Minnie.

'It?' said Major.

'Uh-uh-uh,' said Tuck.

'Not yet,' said Rodney, for the next bit of sorcery was tricky and could quickly get quirky. 'Before you do anything else, let's put a bubble of silence around those other meddling moggies.'

Well, if all the fear in the room had come from Tuck before, the situation soon changed as both Rodney and Janice made their way to the other cage, joined hands and started chanting:

'Beast and bird, insect, crustacean,
All bad things of every nation,
Be as silent as a good relation
And heard no more after this incantation.'

Then, before Ginger could even open her mouth to say it was a terrible spell, the two witches clapped their free hands against each other and drew a large circle around the cage, leaving behind a wobbling semitransparent bubble of glass. From his cage Tuck could see through the bubble to where the other three cats were still talking to one another, but he couldn't hear a word they were saying. In less than a minute they'd gone from mewing to mute, sassy to silent, noisy to, er, not noisy.

'Miaowww,' Tuck miaowed again sadly. 'Oh miaow!'

Then he too fell dumb as Janice approached his cage, reached inside, and hauled him out by the scruff of his neck.

'Are you ready?' she asked Rodney again.

'Nearly,' said Rodney. 'Just remember: as soon as we have him in the pot, anything that is said will become true. We have to be very careful, so listen: this is what's going to happen. We put him in the pot and pat him. Then we pour the boiling pant mixture over him. Then we get each of the other kitties one by one and dice them into the mixture. Then I read out the full spell. Then, when the steam clears, you will have your Purrari, my dear. So remember, once he's in the pot, whatever we say will happen by magic—so say *nothing* but the spell. Got it?'

'Got it!' said Janice, beaming, her black-and-yellow teeth glistening in harmony with the orangey fog around her. She put a clawed and crooked finger to her lips and nodded silently. Then, still carrying Tuck by the scruff of his neck, she followed Rodney into the kitchen. The fog was at its thickest here, and both witches coughed and wafted their arms in front of them so they could see where they were going. Soon they'd cleared the fog enough so that a huge, empty cooking pot became visible on the kitchen counter. Beside it, on the stove, boiled the oil of Rodney's loyal toil.

If Tuck had been able to turn and look into the living room at that point, he'd have seen Minnie and Major, Major and Ginger, Ginger and Minnie throwing themselves against the side of their cage, trying to topple it and smash the silence bubble that surrounded them. He'd have seen the cage wibble and wobble and nearly topple as the weight of three grown cats was hurled against its one side. But he could not turn and see this, and of course he could not hear them either. For Tuck was in the rare state of absolute calm which cats achieve when meditating in the sunlight or when held by the scruff of their necks. All noise and confusion is gone, and suddenly all becomes utterly clear. Scruff-held cats can hear and see and taste and smell perfectly well—it's just that they cannot react. And it is in this state of non-reaction that they have the clearest thoughts.

'I do not want boiling pant juice tipped over me,' thought Tuck in a slightly deeper voice than he normally thought in. 'I do not want to see Ginger and Major and that pretty fluffy one sliced and diced.'

And then he didn't think much else as he found himself popped into the pot and very firmly patted on the head by Rodney. He didn't think, but he did act. As Rodney's hand came in once more for a 'just in case' third pat, Tuck turned and sank his teeth deeply into the soft flesh between Rodney's thumb and the rest of his hand.

'**Aaaagh**!' screamed Rodney. 'Blooming, flipping, bleeding shells, that hurts!'

Tuck jumped out of the pot as fast as he could and was amazed to find on the kitchen counter a hundred small shells, each of them with little flowers blossoming on their sides. They were turning little somersaults over and over until their shells bled.

'You stupid pig!' shouted Janice at Rodney, and can you guess what happened then?

That's right. Rodney Burringo turned into a pig. He stood there, snorting and snuffling on the kitchen floor, looking up at Janice angrily.

'Oh rats!' said Janice, and then she screamed as she found herself surrounded by rats running every which way across the kitchen floor.

Tuck stayed on the kitchen counter, suddenly hungry but not knowing what he should do. 'Er,' he said, desperately trying to think of something clever. 'Er . . . um . . . er.'

'I'm turning on that vacuum cleaner!' screeched Janice, and as she and Tuck stared at each other, they heard the vacuum start up in the living room.

Janice stepped gingerly over the rats, who were running every which way across the floor, and a second later reappeared holding the dreaded vacuum cleaner. But before she could threaten Tuck with it, he thought to himself really loudly at the front of his brain where he couldn't help but listen.

'Being brave doesn't mean not being scared,' he thought.

And without a second thought he jumped down, ran towards Janice and the dreaded dust sucker, and sank his teeth into its inflated bag.

Well, have you ever seen what happens to a balloon when you blow it up and let it go before tying it up? That's what happened to the vacuum cleaner now. It went flying back into the living room and started zooming around in random directions. And as Janice was still holding onto the handle, she went flying around the room with it, banging against walls, smashing into the ceiling, zooming through the yellow fog. And of course everything that Janice shouted out whilst this was happening suddenly appeared in the apartment: a boatload of blistering barnacles, a small dam, piles and piles of dog poo. All of it piled up in the living room as Janice went hurtling around in the air, Rodney the pig chasing her and snorting at the top of his piggy voice.

Then, just as suddenly as it had started flying around, the vacuum cleaner got caught up in the curtains and crashed down, smashing the silence bubble around the other cats' cage and adding its million glistening smithereens to the mess on the living room floor. Ironically, given the silence bubble was now burst, a strange silence fell upon the living room. Small wafts of yellow fog still hung in the air, and they were joined by tiny clouds of dust and canine faecal matter. No one said a word; even Rodney the pig stopped snorting as he looked at where the vacuum cleaner had fallen. For it had fallen heavily, landing right on top of Janice's head, and now she lay still underneath it, her skinny limbs stretched out and her torn cloak revealing a little more leg than anyone was comfortable with. All was still and silent.

Then Janice moved. First of all, a green claw was raised in the air. It was followed by a green finger, then a hand, and then a whole arm. Then all of Janice rose out of the smelly hellish pile of mess. She rose up like a cloud of fury, three metres tall and bending to fit in under the ceiling. The angriest, foulest, most disgustingly angry witch you have never seen in your life. The claw she had first moved had grown a full fifty centimetres long with anger, and she now pointed it across the breakfast bar and into the kitchen at Tuck. Then she opened her mouth to reveal that her teeth had sharpened into fangs oozing with pus. A pungent black gas seeped out between her teeth, filling the room with its stench, and as she opened her mouth her lips drew back to reveal her gums, which had turned into a writhing mess of maggots.

But before Janice could speak, Ginger shouted from the cage, "Witches and pigs turn into rugby balls with feelings! Cages and all doors open! All magic in this room finishes!"

It was a complicated command, and all could feel the magic in the room thinking about it. But the spell from the magazine was powerful, and so the spell rushed towards Janice and Rodney-the-pig in a thick ball of golden light.

But what is more powerful than even a powerful spell? An angry witch is what. And there had never been a witch angrier than Janice Burringo was just at that moment. She flicked off the ball of magic with the back of her hand so that it rolled into a corner that hadn't been dusted since Arthur left.

Then Janice raised her long, evil claw and pointed it at Ginger. 'Die!' she screeched. 'Die slowly and horribly and awfully!' And a hideous neon pink stream of evil trailed out from her claw towards Ginger. The pink neon was a ray of cruel and callous killing. It sparked and crackled and hissed as it travelled through the air, shooting off tiny pink sparks, which might sound pretty but any one of which would kill you in an instant. On and on through the last wisps of yellow fog the cable extended, but when it was halfway across the room Major threw himself on top of Ginger.

'I'll take it,' he shouted. 'You've suffered enough, my love!'

And then possibly the most unexpected thing in this entire story happened. Tuck raced across the living room and threw himself on top of Major. 'Me,' he said. 'I'll take it. You two have wanted to be together for so long.' Tuck closed his eyes tight and tried reminding himself he was brave now.

Still the pink cable of cruelty came towards them, spitting death and looking quite tacky in that way pink neon always does. It had almost reached the pile of Ginger under Major under Tuck when Minnie, probably because she'd been unmentioned for too long in this scene, threw herself on top of Tuck and whispered, 'Don't worry, gorgeous. This one's mine.'

All four cats lay there wide-eyed with fear (apart

from Ginger, who was wide-eyed with the weight of three pussies on top of her) and wondered what the dickens would happen next. But none of them could have imagined it. For none of them knew there is a force in the world more powerful than even the angriest witch. More powerful even than a witch with the most powerful resources at her disposal.

That power is love, and sacrificing yourself for someone else is the greatest expression of that power. You might want to remember that next time it's not your turn to load the dishwasher but you could do it anyway.

Anyhoo, the pink death ray continued to approach, and then, at last, it reached the pile of pussies with a crinkly crackle and hiss. Minnie cringed and Ginger whinged as it singed Minnie's fringe a dingy tinge of orange, and then they all watched as it hinged back upon itself and started heading back towards Janice.

'No!' screamed Janice, flailing her massive arms, trying to shake the start of the cable off her claw and banging her head on the ceiling.

'Oink!' said Rodney, stepping slightly further away from Janice.

The two of them started feeling their way slowly backwards. Neither dared to take their yellow-slash-piggy eyes off the spitting pink death spell, and so neither of them noticed until the very last minute that the corner of the room behind them was bathed in a strange and shifting golden light.

'**Noo**!' screeched Janice again.

'**Oink**!' oinked Rodney.

Only then did the two of them look away from the approaching pink cable of death to Ginger's original command, which sat glowing behind them in the corner of the room. As the cats watched, the stupid pig and the gigantic witch glanced back and forth, forth and back, trapped between an agonising death and life as a rugby ball with feelings. And then—as if they had reached an unspoken agreement—Janice raised her clawed hand and Rodney raised a trotter, and trotter-in-claw they turned and threw themselves onto the golden ball of light.

THE LAST BIT MAYBE

Well, I know what you're expecting. You're expecting something like 'They all lived happily ever after' or 'Ginger and Major got married, and so did Tuck and Minnie' or 'Let's set this up for a sequel just in case it's popular'. And for once (at last!) you are right.

Ginger and Major will get married, but they haven't yet. Major says he won't marry Ginger until she gets her six bellies back because that was what he was missing for all those years, and he doesn't want some toned-up, slimmed-down version of his long-lost love stopping his dreams from coming true. As you can imagine, he won't have to wait too long. These days Ginger simply sits around the stables all day, bossing people about and asking for more food. Major's so content to have her home he's more than happy to run around after her, at least he is for some of the day. When he gets bored of it, he simply finds a spot in the sun which no one else knows about, applies his selective hearing, and meditates with his eyes tightly shut.

As for Minnie and Tuck, well, it's been a match made in heaven. Minnie is no less annoying than ever, but Tuck doesn't seem to care. Tuck just loses himself in his memories of mushroom sauce. Meanwhile, Minnie miaows on about how fat Ginger is getting, how dull

Major is these days, and how pretty she is. Especially about how pretty she is, to tell the truth. And when she gets bored of that, she jumps on Tuck, and they wrestle and fight and chase each other around the farmyard until they are both out of breath.

But the cats didn't get to the stables until a couple of weeks after they'd survived the Burringos' death spell. First of all, they had to find a cleaning company (Arthur's Global Cleaning Corp., Inc.) prepared to clear the Burringos' apartment of dog poo, rats, barnacles, and broken glass (not to mention a huge pile of toenails they found under the sofa). But the most difficult part was getting rid of the rugby balls which Ginger had turned the Burringos into. Initially, Major took them to a local rugby club, but after a while he got a phone call saying he had to pick them up again.

'They keep saying, "OUCH!" every time we kick them,' said the club captain. 'It's most off-putting.'

Then Ginger tried donating them to a local school, but again they were handed back.

'They complain when we land on them in the mud,' said one of the teachers. 'And they do it in the foulest language. I really cannot have our pupils exposed to such crassness.'

Finally, Minnie had a bright idea which the other three cats agreed couldn't be beat. They donated the balls to the Try, Try and Try Again Rugby School for the Deaf. There at last the balls were happily accepted, and as far as anyone knows, there they are still kicked and thrown and jumped on in the mud on a daily basis.

And just as long as no one ever rubs them three times anticlockwise in a rainstorm while saying, 'Catch these balls, then kick your bum, this magic shall be undone', there they will stay forever.

So let's hope that doesn't happen, eh?

THE END

Or is it?

If you enjoyed *Cats On The Run* and you'd like to hear about Tuck and Ginger's next adventure, go to
www.tuckandginger.com

Made in the USA
Middletown, DE
09 July 2018